American Teenagers.sys

American Teenagers.sys

A Time-Travel Novel

Eugene C. Rideout

iUniverse, Inc.
New York Bloomington

American Teenagers.sys
A Time-Travel Novel

iUniverse books may be ordered through booksellers or by contacting:

iUniverse
1663 Liberty Drive
Bloomington, IN 47403
www.iuniverse.com
1-800-Authors (1-800-288-4677)

ISBN: 978-1-4401-4619-0 (pbk)
ISBN: 978-1-4401-4612-1 (dj)
ISBN: 978-1-4401-4620-6 (ebk)

Printed in the United States of America

iUniverse rev. date: 5/26/2009

1 The Missouri Rifleman

The stream of .30-caliber bullets rockets out of the plasma TV, miraculously missing the right arm of the lone young viewer.

The damage to the sofa is massive indeed. The entire right arm is shattered, which renders that end of the seat barely usable.

Severely shocked by the projectiles that have buried themselves in a shower of wood splinters in the lumber frame of the four seater where his arm had been resting, fifteen-year-old David James Richardson gasps.

The grade ten prodigy stabs at the buttons on the remote control he is using to surf for a program to watch. Now, "I've got to turn this thing off, so that doesn't happen again!" he mutters to himself under his breath.

The intent is to prevent further shots from blasting out of the family's entertainment center. "Bullets can't get out of the TV and damage furniture; things like that don't happen," he stammers aloud.

He punches at the touch-screen of the set's remote control, but quickly realizes that, in the clumsiness of his panic, rather than hitting the OFF button, he has instead pressed the ▲COMPASS button.

The image of what appears to be a World War II American soldier or marine does not disappear. Instead, DJ is almost petrified when the M1-Garand-rifle-toting serviceman suddenly zooms in to point-blank range.

For the first time in its history, the Richardson's family room is penetrated by the business end of a firearm.

"Don't shoot!" the boy yells.

Instantly, almost without a thought, he begins to poke repeatedly at the ▼COMPASS button to reverse the action that brought the uniformed man up close and personal, right into the home of the St. Petersburg, Florida, family.

He is delighted to see the warrior rapidly, although at first only in a brief series of jerky movements; then, thankfully, as far as James is concerned, smoothly, totally back off from his earlier confrontational stance, as the boy deliberately holds the button down.

His huge sigh of relief is clearly audible at the immediacy of the troop withdrawal from his home.

A distinct lack of daylight in the scene causes the teenager some difficulty seeing much beyond one hundred yards or so.

His thoughts revert once more to turning off the set his dad has recently installed in the family's rec room.

However, it occurs to Deej, before he hits the OFF button, that nobody will ever believe his story in a month of Sundays.

If the lad powers down the TV, he will destroy virtually every scrap of evidence he has of the momentous incident. Everything, that is, with the exception of the enormous holes gouged into the settee.

So, there is an urgent need to get a second opinion.

What an intriguing and challenging decision the teen needs to make.

He must choose between getting verification of what he has seen and experienced, or, pulling the plug, and thus powering off the set, losing everything.

The damning thing, it, is that the proof of the reality of his experience lies in leaving the TV on and letting someone else see it.

From his family's experiences, the teen knows instinctively that the intruder is an American warrior; probably from World War II. He cannot conjure up any additional information that would explain the strange, violent intrusion.

All of this prompts many questions: Should DJ fear an increase of danger presented by this, or other armed men entering the house through the HD device?

Perhaps even more importantly, will he be able to control whatever happens next?

If James leaves the set on will it continue responding in a similar way?

#

"Life is great," is not an expression he is about to use; especially now, after this experience.

School is out for James. It is just before 5:00 p.m. on Saturday, February 21, 2015.

Heavy clouds are contributing nothing toward making this a fun day.

Rain, heavy at times, frequently attended by lightning and its resulting thunder, has not allowed the lad to be an active participant in anything outside the house.

Normally, a sunny Saturday would be taken up with sports, like baseball or soccer.

Today would not give you the impression that this Florida resort city is able to advertise an average of three hundred and sixty days of sunshine each year.

Now, as the gloom of a mid-winter nightfall begins to set in, compounded by the stormy skies above his home, the youngster is waiting for his parents to arrive from the airport.

DJ's folks are returning from spending their Friday keeping business appointments, and most of Saturday making family visits in Atlanta, Georgia.

Alone in the house with his older sister, Lyndsey, herself a near-prodigy sixteen-year-old high-school senior, it occurs to the lad that what has just occurred is well beyond fantastic.

No, not the experience alone; that had proven to be phenomenal.

Rather, the feeling returns to him that by means of a television set, although for but a few moments, the ability to become involved in real-time history has briefly become a possibility for him.

Having ex-military men in the inner circle of his close-knit family, the boy knows enough about the armed forces of the United States to quickly recognize the appearance of American warriors from the various eras.

This includes both World Wars I and II, as well as Korea, and Vietnam.

Like the uniforms of the American Civil War, each of those later conflicts had its own distinctive uniform style, easily recognizable to the discerning eye despite the passage of time.

So, somehow, Dad's new television has permitted a physical interaction, between the present day in 2015, and the very far distant past of the Second World War.

These thoughts quickly jell in his mind to make Deej realize he has no choice!

"Lynz!" he cries, "come here, quick!"

Alerted by the sound of gunfire, and James' scream at the marine warrior, Lyndsey Parker Richardson is already en route from her third-floor bedroom to the family room.

As the senior teen present, she feels a need to investigate the cause of the racket her brother is generating.

"What's all the yelling about?" she demands. The questioning look on her face tells the story. She slowly descends the stairs to the living room.

"Why are you screaming? … What on earth was that shooting?

"For the love of Pete! What in the world have you done to the daybed, David James Richardson?" she challenges the fifteen-year-old by his full nomenclature, staring incredulously at the mangled piece of furniture.

Normally the two share an excellent relationship, but this is too much.

"Just wait till Dad sees what you've done to this sofa," she chides.

"Who cares about the chair," the boy retorts. "Take a look at this!"

Having little more than a crude idea as to what effect it might have, DJ slowly and deliberately presses the ▲COMPASS button, even doubting within himself that it will again function as it had before.

Mixed feelings of happiness — it has to be more like vindication, in reality — and fear overwhelm him as he sees, in the half-light of that dawn battlefield scene, the far-off marine slowly yet distinctly getting closer.

He stops before the armed combatant gets within effective range.

"I don't see a thing," the girl insists.

Suddenly realizing something that will help him resolve his problems with the doubters later, James slips a new, blank DVD into the recording device attached to the TV and starts the machine, to get a permanent record of whatever happens during the next confrontation, should there be one.

"Still nothing," the girl harps.

Totally unimpressed at the sight of yet another soldier on the TV, and far away, at that, she asks herself, "Why are the males of this household so fascinated with military things?"

Still intensely annoyed over the massive damage to the piece of furniture, she blurts out: "You're not showing me anything, DJ. How did our davenport get smashed?"

"He did it!" DJ has trouble containing himself, and excitedly gestures in the direction of the U.S. military man he can see on the TV.

Infuriated, Lyndsey resorts to ridicule: "What have you been smoking?"

This is a ludicrous rhetorical question, but she is trying to illustrate for James, that his constantly putting blame on the far distant marine is idiotic, and makes no sense whatsoever.

"It can't have been him," she lectures. "TVs don't do that sort of thing. They can't just run off and show whatever they want; they can only display the programs the TV stations put out!

"So, David James, that leaves you; what did you do to our sofa?"

"Good grief, Lynz," he says, "I'll zoom this guy in again and you can see for yourself what happened!"

Although subconsciously he feels a desperate need to be cautious, he is being forced into rapidly shedding his inhibitions.

His sister's relentless pressure is beginning to get to him.

Once more, the young student stabs at the ▲COMPASS button repeatedly, finally holding the button down for a brief period.

The Marine private looms larger and larger, until he pulls in so close that the wood-sheathed barrel of his rifle again sticks right out of the TV, a full twelve inches into the room.

Lyndsey screams, "Stop, James!" reacting with shock at this development, having never been exposed to such war weaponry before.

"Sorry I busted a cap at y'all, sir," the young steel-helmeted stranger drawls. "I dun thought y'all wuz the enemy; it's a good thing I heard y'all a-speakin' English. Everything is so damned hostile here on Iwo Jima.

"I'm just a farm boy from Clay County, Missouri, trying to stay alive in this here pesky war! That tends to make you shoot at anything unfamiliar … Please pardon my French, ma'am.

"I don't see any way that we can ever win this here battle; it just seems to go on endlessly. We landed at 9:00 a.m. day before yesterday, February 19, and the shooting hasn't stopped since we dun arrived!

"Who are you people, anyway? … How did y'all get here? … What are y'all a-doin' here? … Don't y'all know we got a war a-goin' on?

"Holy smokes! What on earth happened to your love seat?"

"I was just surfing through the channels on our TV, sir, and suddenly you appeared. The chair was wrecked when it was hit by bullets from your rifle. I'm sorry I alarmed you and made you shoot."

"Y'all were doing what? ... What in creation is a TV?" he demands; but suddenly interjects, "I have to go; my sergeant is a-callin'."

"Before you go, sir! What place did you say this is? Where are we again?"

"This here is the Japanese island of Iwo Jima; it means *Sulfur Island*. We are about 750 miles from Tokyo.

"See y'all later, folks!" At this, his rifle is withdrawn without further incident from the HD screen of their dad's favorite toy.

The two Richardsons exchange the thought that the Missourian looks incredibly young as he lopes off in his camouflaged outfit to rejoin his squad.

Now Lyndsey watches studiously, and with a much more intense level of interest, as her brother again backs off from the area using the ▼COMPASS button.

As the view slowly fades of the now well-lit background, she notes, with his agreement, that the overall scene is that of a huge battlefield located on a small, partly flat, island.

Its most prominent features is that, aesthetically it is unbalanced; completely dominated at one end by an unusual looking mountain about five hundred feet high; probably, the girl adds, an extinct volcano.

"Lynz, that marine has no idea what a TV is! … How could that be? … What planet is he from?"

"Deej," she asks, ignoring his questions, "what do you think would happen if you tried pressing a different button on the remote?"

The question brings renewed feelings of trepidation to the lad.

"Lynz, this is not a game, you know," he cautions. "What happens if we get up close and you get shot?"

The girl continues her quest, "Well, just take it easy! Go slowly! Be ready to reverse whatever you do."

"Hey, hold on! You've tried the forward and the reverse; now try the left and right buttons and press them only once or twice, just in case. Go slowly!"

At that crucial moment, the doorbell rang, insistently, twice.

"DJ, just let me get rid of whoever's at the door and I'll be back; wait for me!"

#

"Oh! Hi! … Grandpa Richardson! What brings you out on a dirty day like this?"

"Hello, Lyndsey. Boy, I'm glad I found somebody at home. I had a late appointment at the hardware store and thought I'd drop by on the way home.

"I just wanted to say hello to you folks. Is your dad home?"

"No, Gramps. They're just flying in from Atlanta; Dad had a few sales calls in the city, and he took Mom with him yesterday morning. Today, they were planning a couple of family visits while they were there.

"They phoned a little earlier to confirm that they had made it to the check-in at Hartsfield and told us we could expect them back here about 7:00 p.m., in a couple of hours."

"What are you two doing? What've you got for homework?"

"Grandpa Buck, our homework is all done; but something very strange just happened with our TV. Could you take a look at it and let us know if you have ever heard of that sort of thing before?"

"Do you mean your dad's new HDTV? Hey, I hope it's not broken."

"No, the set's OK, Gramps; it's what just came on it that's upsetting us!"

"Whaddya mean?"

"Come down to the rec room and DJ can show you what happened to us just now."

"James, it's Grandpa Buck!" the girl calls down the stairs.

"Hey, DJ; how's it going? Lynz tells me something unusual happened to your TV. Holy crow! What on earth's damaged your sofa like that?"

"Well, I was just surfing on the TV for something to watch and this happened, Gramps."

The youngster presses on the button that, a little earlier, caused the island to loom large on the HDTV, and zips in to the area where the young Missourian had appeared previously.

This time, however, the young American warrior is nowhere in sight.

"Seriously, Granddad, I zoomed in on an American soldier and gave him a scare, and he fired his rifle into our daybed! He only just missed me!"

The combat zone is filled with the never-ending sights and sounds of fierce battle, the crackle and roar of out-of-control fires, and multiple explosions.

To be prudent, he backs off from the scene until the coastline of the island with its blob of a volcano away in the distance is all that remains in sight.

Buckminster Richardson needs to see no more. Although born in 1957, years after the war ended, he proclaims dogmatically, "That's Iwo Jima. That's what it looked like back in 1945.

"I recognize Mount Suribachi at the far end.

"What you see there, Deej, is the east side of the island, where the U.S. military landed its troops for the invasion.

"My, what a fight the Marines had for that tiny chunk of real estate, let me tell you!

"My granddad, that's your great-great-grandfather, was drafted into the U.S. Army back then, and he fought against the Japanese in the Pacific.

"I'll bet that what you've found is some history program that is showing old footage of the fighting for Iwo."

"You're right about the island. The marine just identified it as Iwo Jima, and told us it is close to Japan, but, Gramps, this is not a TV program.

"This is live! That's the strange thing that's happening to Dad's new television!"

"It can't be live, son; TVs don't do that sort of thing. They can't just run off and show whatever they want; they can only display the programs the TV stations put out!"

"So far, you're the third one to say that. We both said exactly the same thing. But that's not true in this case.

"Look!" As he speaks, Deej 'gasses up' the big TV and 'drives' it in to Iwo Jima again. Somehow, James has to prove to his grandfather that his own earlier statements are accurate and true.

He moves the screen view to display the area where the initial confrontations had taken place.

At first, he again finds only scenes of battle; more thunderous explosions, the constant rattle of innumerable small arms.

These will not convince his grandfather of anything. To the older Richardson it still looks like a regular history program being shown on TV.

Lynz had been a tough nut to crack, but she finally saw the light. Now Gramps has to become a convert too.

"James! Look! That's the guy from Missouri; over there, on the right!"

"See, Gramps. There he is!" echoes her brother. "That's the marine who shot up our sofa!"

He can now point out to his grandfather the warrior his sister has identified, sprawled out on the near side of a large boulder.

The marine is firing his rifle at a Japanese soldier.

The diminutive enemy is carrying what looks like a Bangalore Torpedo to be used to clear a small group of American soldiers armed with flamethrowers off a small rise in the terrain.

Deej cruises in close to the Missouri lad, "Can we help, sir?" he calls out.

"You know, I can barely see y'all, folks; and we might be able to make use of that.

"Would it be possible for y'all to carry me across to that huge rock over there?" he drawls.

"If I'm having trouble spotting y'all, it may be that the Japanese are not able to eyeball us either, and I may be able to get off a few shots at that guy."

"Sure! Climb right in."

The young marine tosses his Garand rifle through the portal into the rec room, quickly following it with his body. Whose jaw drops? ... Buckminster Richardson!

The polished floor does not fare well at the hands of the marine combatant.

A Garand tips the scales at over 9 lbs. The multiple steel parts on it leave many more dents in the shiny floor than do the marine's hands and knees.

"OK. That rock over there, just about fifty yards out. If y'all could take me there, that would be swell."

James complies quickly without a word.

LP and her grandfather are speechless at this turn of events, but nonetheless they continue to pay rapt attention to the goings-on.

The youthful combatant, complete with rifle, rapidly exits through the HD screen, not realizing that this is really a time machine.

Its likes he has never seen before, and, in all probability, will never see again.

From the haven of the large rock, the marine blasts away an entire eight-round magazine. The empty clip automatically ejects with its very distinctive 'ping' sound.

"I dun missed the son of a gunner," he exclaims, for the second time heaving his Garand through the screen onto the Richardson's wood floor; naturally, causing ever more dents.

His average-sized frame follows and he draws himself up to his full 5 feet, 9 inches and moans, "For some reason those cartridges were like they wuz duds!

"I could see the bullets just a-fallin' out of the end of the barrel of my rifle. I can't believe that; eight misfires out of eight rounds!

"Anyway, I appreciate y'all a-helpin', folks. Say, remind me again, what was it that happened to your chair?"

Lynz speaks as DJ 'drives' back to the young marine's original location, "It's a long story."

"Thanks for your help, folks."

"Who are you, sir? What is your name?" Lyndsey inquires of the uniformed man.

"Bartlett James, Jr. of the Clay County James family, ma'am. Thank you again for your help."

Gathering up his Garand, he clambers through the TV, for the third and final time, to disappear into the broad daylight of an Iwo Jima morning.

Buckminster confessed, "Deej, I'm so sorry I doubted your word. I've neither seen, nor heard, anything remotely like that, on TV or anywhere else. What an incredible experience."

As the older Richardson speaks these words, DJ pulls back from the heavily contested area until, once again, the east coast is the only part of the island that remains visible. Mount Suribachi is still obscured by the incessant, heavy naval artillery fire.

Lynz responds to Buck's comment by expressing her own thoughts on the matter, questioning where the phenomenon originated.

"Who sent this portal to us? No one else has this capability with his or her TV.

"Is it from heaven, or the angels? I can't think of any other source for it. Who has this capability, and is able to pass it on to others?"

#

"Gramps, when you rang the doorbell, Lynz and I were just about to try a couple of experiments to find out if we are able to change the view.

"We know we can move in and out from a scene, but we want to see if we can move around in other directions."

"Hey, don't let me stop you, kids. This is fascinating."

Iwo Jima is still in sight in the distance, and, with one finger poised to get out of whatever he does, James pokes at the ►COMPASS button.

The result seems negligible. The volcanic island appears to move very slightly to the left.

A digit to the ◄COMPASS button simply causes the Pacific rock to move back to its original position, and a second push of the ◄COMPASS button takes the island fortress an additional tiny notch further to the right.

A third finger-press on the same button has an identical effect.

"Deej, try holding that button down … to see if it repeats that movement," the girl suggests.

A steady press on the ◄COMPASS button now causes the Japanese-held island to move, slowly at first, then smoothly, then rapidly, from the center of their view until it almost disappears from sight off the right hand side of the screen.

All that now remains in sight is the deep blue Pacific Ocean with hundreds of ships of every imaginable size, shape, and purpose, either at anchor or moving around near that island coastline.

"Look at all those ships. What in the world can a fleet of that size be doing?" the boy queries.

Granddad breaks in, "If you're able to move left and right like that, why don't you navigate over there, and let's all have a look."

The boy uses the remote, and, pressing the touch-pad keys he has already experimented with, moves Gramps, his sibling, and himself, in closer to the action that is taking place offshore of the embattled Iwo.

Drawing in to within a half mile of the closest capital ship, the three can see the whole of a large naval squadron, sporting a number of huge aircraft carriers. The war birds from the flattops are lending much needed ground-support fire to the Marine grunts on the island.

Included too, are six massive battleships, a number of cruisers, and, finally, many destroyers, all using their huge rifled guns.

Amid a dreadful roar, the continue landing salvo after salvo of shells on the slopes of Mount Suribachi, the strange-looking igneous-extrusion-like hill at the southern (Tobiishi Point) end of Iwo Jima.

Other U.S. landing craft and many other small boats can be seen packed with men heading for the island battlefront.

If he could turn in his grave, Ferdinand Magellan, the Portuguese explorer, who died in 1521 CE, undoubtedly would surely do that.

The Pacific Ocean is called thus from its title in Latin, "Mare Pacificum," or, "peaceful sea," an appellation given to it by Magellan himself.

There is no mistaking this for a "peaceful sea," here offshore of the 8-square-mile island.

"Kids, it's hard to believe that this is really happening." Once again, Buckminster expresses his feelings of wonderment at what his grandchildren have shown him by means of the high-definition set.

"Listen," Buck's excitement about James' discovery shows. "You've already figured out how to close in and back off from a scene, and you just worked out how to move from side to side.

"Now, this is up to you, guys, but how would you feel about trying some of the other buttons on the remote; like the ▲CH or ▼CH, or the ▲VOL and ▼VOL?

"Go easy when you press them. Just be ready to reverse any effect that you think may not be desirable."

"Gramps, I just got through telling Lynz we could get ourselves killed if we wind up on the wrong end of somebody's gun again!"

"Yes, I recognize that, DJ, but, what I reckon is that things are falling into place far too easily here. What I'm thinking is that every button that you've tried so far has had a logical function attached to it.

"Don't forget what just happened to Bartlett James a few minutes ago. He had eight consecutive misfires on his M-1. Now, exactly what, or who, made that happen?

"Is Lynz right? Has this fascinating portal been sent to you by some higher power? Maybe by someone who hates violence. I'm just wondering if this goes any farther.

"Because there just seems to be some sort of order to all of this.

"If you'd be willing to try it out, it may be that you'll find other effects that are going to help you to make better use of this system, or machine, or capability, or gizmo, or whatever it is."

Thus is born the title by which this phenomenon has come to be called, and will in future be known, the ***System***.

"Well, I'll tell you, the more I think about doing this, I sure wish I had a gun, that's all!"

"How would you feel about shooting one of our marines?" Buckminster questions.

"I sure wouldn't want to do that, Gramps."

"Listen, even though it's still broad daylight through the set, just remember what Bartlett James said about the visibility of the portal. It's not very likely those folks on the ships or the island will be able to see us anyway.

"Just be ready to backpedal out of anything undesirable you get into, and remember, take it easy!" Buck encourages.

"You still have to try out the ▲CH or ▼CH buttons yet, Deej," Lyndsey prompts.

In response to his sister's suggestion, James asks Lynz if she would keep notes of any buttons he pushes. There must be no case of "I don't remember," attached to this operation.

They both know that future use of the *System* may rely on good records from these early activities.

Granddad wears a smug smile, while Lyndsey, notepad in hand, peers inquiringly over DJ's shoulder; and the lad prepares to start pressing buttons.

Deej, continuing the earlier conversation, "I tend to agree, Gramps. Every push of these buttons convinces me more that Lynz may be right, and this is some kind of gift. Anyway, here goes with the ▲CH button. Ready, Lynz?"

"I'm with you."

Now, on the left side of the remote, "▲CH button: one push ... Did anyone see anything happen?"

Lyndsey, "It looks to me like a video that has skipped. What do you think, Granddad?"

"I agree with your sister, Deej, it looks like a piece of movie film that has been joined too many times.

"Try that again; only hold the button down this time. Gently, take it easy."

"▲CH: Down, and hold!"

"Look at the ships scurrying around; it's like time-lapse photography. Hey! It's getting dark already."

"Granddad Buck, that's not a projection effect; that's us! We're moving forward in time! Let me go the other way with the ▼CH.

"I hope you're right about there being some sort of order to this ... Awesome! ... It works too!" the boy chortles.

"It's getting lighter! ... The whole scene is moving backward again ... now forward ... now backward ... then forward once more ... it's high speed motion, Gramps, but still live action."

Lyndsey exclaims, "This is spectacular! There really is organization to this!

"What in heaven's name is going on? Why is this happening to us?

"We're able to make the TV travel through time. Gramps, did you say you had heard of this happening to someone else?"

Buckminster confessed, "No, Lynz, just the opposite. I have never heard of anyone with a capability like this before.

"But I'd be willing to bet there are billions of people who wish they could have it, though."

Now, in an episode that comes upon them without warning, in sudden horror the trio watches helplessly as six Japanese *kamikaze* pilots, carry out a suicide attack on one of the flattops.

Taking advantage of low-cloud cover, they plunge their bomb-laden airplanes toward a large aircraft carrier and five of them succeed in deliberately crashing onto her decks.

The sixth craft is disintegrated by anti-aircraft fire, from the guns of the picket line of destroyers set up as an outlying guard against such attacks.

Unfortunately, although the physical damage to the ship itself is not severe, the raid, at 5:00 p.m., costs the lives of one hundred and twenty-three of her crew.

DJ 'drives' backward in time once more to the beginning of the *kamikaze* attack, then backs up briefly and advances slowly to the stern end of the huge aircraft carrier where the name *Saratoga* is displayed in huge letters.

For safety's sake, James moves slightly ahead in time, to avoid possible harm to his family from future attacks on the flattop.

"My goodness! What on earth have you found here, Deej, Lynz?" Buck exclaims, still in wonder.

Because the enormous fleet is such an awesome sight, the siblings and their granddad spend quite some time cruising around the area of the Pacific island, watching the ships of the Iwo Jima task force mostly at anchor.

With DJ's help, Lyndsey takes turns 'driving' the *System* around the ships.

She practices moving in time, both forward and backward, to be able to locate different scenes, until she becomes quite adept at making changes.

The trio marvels at aircraft take-off and touchdown operations, crowds of landing craft circling in the wake of their mother ships.

It is intriguing to the kids how the planes and boats are able to move around, in the sky, or on the sea, respectively, without ever crashing into each other.

Buckminster, an ex military officer, knows the long hours, days, weeks, and months of practice that go into making such operations run smoothly.

So, both DJ and Lyndsey make use of this opportunity to give each other suggestions on how to 'drive' the portal around the fleet.

They watch the ships and small boats carrying personnel moving around.

The larger ships are going about their business; the landing craft shuttling scores upon scores of men from ship to shore.

Each vessel is making the most of the approach of darkness for cover from enemy fire originating on the island.

The experience the siblings are getting piloting the device around using the remote control will later prove to be of benefit in another sense.

They still have to demonstrate the discovery to others to prove that their eyewitness accounts are true, and, eventually, also in their experimental activities.

Still on the left side of the remote: "OK ▲VOL, Lynz." The boy presses just once. "Nothing!"

"Press it two or three times; if that does nothing then hold it down!" comes from the grey-headed one.

"Ooooo-eeeee! Look at us go up in the air! Look at the lights on those ships! This is better than being in a helicopter."

"Now make it go down again, James." Lyndsey directs. "Easy ... go slowly! It's hard to see the ocean in this light ... You don't want us to go swimming, do you?"

James releases the ▼VOL button, and the *System*, as Buckminster Richardson has unofficially named it, settles down just three or four feet above the surface of the Pacific Ocean.

"Granddad Buck, you were right; each of the buttons we've tried so far has its own function."

Lyndsey voices a profound conclusion, "Do you realize the meaning of what the three of us are witnessing here?

"According to what Deej just did, we can watch *Saratoga* being attacked, as many times as we want, always live ... and we appear to have access to things that happened a long time ago.

"But, each time we watch something, it is as if it is just occurring for the very first time.

"The *System* is allowing us to travel through time to 1945; three-quarters of a century ago.

"From what you said, Gramps, no-one has ever done that before." she says.

[Through their mobile phones, from Internet Web pages, a little later, the folks discover the official Navy record of this *kamikaze* attack, which lasted only three minutes.

The action actually started at 5:00 p.m. on February 21, 1945, on USS *Saratoga*, a flattop built from what was intended to be a battle-cruiser hull, and commissioned by the U.S. Navy in 1927.

This seemingly insignificant detail is not presented as trivia, but rather, as vitally important and meaningful data. It establishes an indent on the yardstick of time for the trio.

It unerringly identifies the point in America's history at which the kids and Buck Richardson have experienced their confrontations with the Clay County, Missouri, marine.

This is awe-inspiring, inasmuch as it verifies for the kids and their granddad that the trio has traversed close to 7,780 miles (each way) of real estate.

Too, they have literally traveled backward in time to a date on the calendar when this country's thirty-second president, Franklin Delano Roosevelt, is alive and well, and serving as Commander-In-Chief of the military forces.

Finally, that they have actually seen young Americans fighting a desperate enemy of the United States; seventy years in the past, back in 1945!]

#

"Kids; this is your call. Ladybird would be thrilled to experience this. Do you think it would be OK if I got her to come to the house so that she can see it too?"

"Well, Gramps, the word is going to get out sooner or later.

"I was hoping we'd be able to keep it on a need-to-know basis, until we've been able to have a word with Dad and Mom, but I don't see what harm it could do if Grandma Ladybuck came and had a look.

"Will you call her and get her to drive herself here?"

"She can call a taxi if she wants to; just as long as she doesn't take too long about it."

#

"Buckminster! What's this all about?" Ladybird Richardson calls out, as she sweeps down the stairs, making a grand entrance. She is in the company of Lyndsey, the designated doorkeeper.

Affectionately known to all as Ladybuck, she is a grand lady who has skillfully blended her school-teaching career with her wifely duties and her other fulltime job, raising their three children.

"Cripes! What's with the sofa?" she gasps, letting go of her college-diploma and masters-degree English-language skills in favor of more readily recognizable vernacular expressions.

Precisely twenty-five minutes have elapsed from the time Buck called his wife, until the ring on the doorbell.

"You won't believe this, darling! Get a load of what happened to Deej and the TV a bit earlier. The kids have been showing me this stuff ever since I came here from my appointment with the consultant at the Hardware Doctor."

"What are you talking about, Buck? What's happened?" she asks impatiently.

"Deej was surfing on Russell's high-def TV a couple of hours ago. I can't figure out what happened.

"There was a lot of lightning and thunder for quite a while earlier and I guess it's always possible that the house was struck by lightning; but it's had a very strange effect on the TV."

"Your point is?"

"Sorry. DJ, can you show Ladybuck the carrier you showed me before?"

"Did you get me all the way over here just to look at an aircraft carrier on TV?" she asks.

"Yes, but you never saw one like this before, my love," Buckminster assures his wife.

Deej again draws the *System* up toward the offshore fleet; changing time slots so that a pristine USS *Saratoga* is once again clearly in sight at point-blank range, close enough to permit Ladybuck to be able to see the crew moving around on her flight deck.

"OK, I'm waiting … What's happening?" she queries yet again. Her patience is beginning to wear thin.

"Oh, my word! What's that smell?" she wants to know. "Is that something in here?"

"That's the ship," Buck explains. "That's the smell of the smoke from the funnel, and the avgas fumes from the aircraft, that are landing and taking off from the carrier."

"What is this, '*Whiff-o-Vision*'? You can't smell things that are on TV."

"Grandma, this isn't an ordinary TV program," Lyndsey explains. "This is not video or old pictures. This is *live*. You're looking at the U.S. fleet offshore of Iwo Jima, during the Second World War.

"Now look at what happens. Watch those six aircraft diving down onto the flight deck of that aircraft carrier. That old flattop is USS *Saratoga* on February 21, today's date, but back in 1945."

"Good grief! Why did they do that?"

"They're *kamikaze* aircraft. The pilots crash their planes onto the carrier to try to sink it. They individually committed suicide in order to do that," the girl continues.

"Each of those aircraft was carrying at least one bomb, so there's no way any of those pilots could have survived. We've watched that attack several times now, live each time."

"How can this happen?" Ladybird exclaims. "It can't be live, guys! TVs don't do that sort of thing. They can't just run off and show whatever they want; they can only display the programs the TV stations put out!"

"Grandma, you're the fourth person to say that today. That's exactly what each one of us thought. But, this is live, and kind of scary, if you ask me?"

As Lyndsey speaks, James again moves forward briefly in time for the sake of their own security.

"Where are your dad and mom? Why is it they're not here with you?"

"Darling, Russ and Dianne are on the way home from a trip to Atlanta," Buck volunteers. "The kids say they'll be here in a little while; about seven o'clock."

"Hey, I can't wait to hear Russell howl when he sees that chair," the older woman grins. "How did it get damaged anyway?"

Again, the story of Bartlett James, the marine from Clay County, Missouri, is related, and another routine inspection of the enormous holes in the sofa takes place.

"Let me understand, are you telling me that this is not on the TV, but rather that I am able to watch it live through the set, as if I am looking at it through a window?"

"Grandma, what a useful illustration. Yes! That's it precisely," DJ commends.

"This is unbelievable," she says. "It's hard to comprehend how something like this could happen."

"Let's hope Dad is as easy to convince as you are, Grandma."

Lyndsey wants to make sure no one misses the point, "I hope you realize what James said about today being February 21, 2015, here in St. Pete's. This is the seventieth anniversary of the 1945 attack on *Saratoga*."

"Say, kids, it's only just after dark at Iwo Jima, but it'll be dark and close to dawn by the time we arrive back home in St. Petersburg. It would probably be a good idea to move backward in time for a few hours. That way we can travel in daylight. You can make a final adjustment when you get the *System* back to St. Pete's."

"Granddad, that sounds like a good suggestion."

Deej reverses the view until it appears to be just after sunrise on Iwo, then turns the *System* onto a northeasterly course until he figures that he will bypass Hawaii on the way back to the United States.

Next, he 'guns' the remote control into forward motion at 'warp speed.'

Thanks to the International Date Line, the 7:00 a.m. time at Iwo Jima turned into 1:00 p.m. the previous day at Honolulu, and it remains daylight for quite a while.

Ladybuck first spots the islands of Hawaii on the right side of the screen.

That verifies, at least, that their vector is in the right direction and so Deej just edges it slightly to the south to insure passage over the North American coastline in the Los Angeles area.

From the Hawaiian Islands area to the California coast takes a lot less than one minute of time. It is 4:00 p.m. The Los Angeles area becomes visible, but there is something strange to the eye. No highways crammed with speeding cars hove into sight.

The terrain below is unbelievably free of urban development; the enormous build-up of the post-war years simply is not there. This obviously is not the Los Angeles of the twenty-first century.

As the homeward journey progresses, DJ stops the *System*, making a slight adjustment to their location in the stream of time.

This is because, while it is 4:00 p.m. Pacific Time in Los Angeles, it is no longer daylight in St Pete's, three hours ahead, on Eastern Standard Time.

The boy makes a minor time reversal to ensure that their hometown arrival will be before sunset, which should be occurring about thirty minutes after touchdown.

It is now a simple matter to make a minor change to their course, and direct the *System* toward the east coast and the Atlantic Ocean.

The quartet arrives in short order over the eastern seaboard expecting to see the Oceana Naval Air Station at Virginia Beach, where the ramp should be crowded with dozens of F-22 Raptor fighter-jets.

Their aircraft-loving eyes would have been richly blessed if their homeward flight could have been slightly interrupted by a slow and deep undulation along Oceana's Runway 05R which, under normal circumstances, provides the best view of the parked fighter jets.

The oscillation might have happened, but, nothing! It isn't there! No Oceana! No jets! Rather, it appears to be a small airfield located on what looks like a scarcely lit farmer's field.

"Ding!" Granddad Richardson has an answer for what has happened: "Got it, guys! What you're looking at here is what will eventually become NAS Oceana, but we're here in 1945; at least, we think it's 1945. The F-22 Raptor is a product of late in the twentieth century, fifty-some years in the future.

"All you're likely to find at Oceana in 1945, if anything, is a supply of Chance-Vought F4U Corsairs."

"Buck! Let me see if I can verify that on the Internet on my phone, and get back to you," Ladybuck offers. She picks up her mobile and strolls off into the hallway to concentrate on the data.

As he climbs up out of the Oceana area, the youngster makes a gentle turn just south of Virginia Beach and 'beetles on down' to Jacksonville, Florida, where the group turns south southwest and crosses the hinterland of Florida toward Tampa Bay.

Because it sprang to public attention between the Spanish-American war and World War I, Orlando is there as a well-developed area, but no sign of the huge theme park that will become such a great contributor to its economy in later years.

Deej and his family are not surprised by the absence of this prominent feature of Central Florida's landscape.

DJ takes the *System* forward across the Bay; past what the history-conscious group by now knows probably is not going to be MacDill Air Force Base, but rather, Southeast Air Base, Tampa.

Tampa Bay passes beneath them in a mere moment and they arrive at the site of the beautiful St. Petersburg pier, although this edifice has yet to be constructed there in decades yet ahead.

Alongside that lay the Albert Whitted Airport, a naval-cadet training station for much of the war-years period.

For generations of pilots not yet born, it will provide take-off and landing services, as well as to many hundreds of thousands of small private aircraft over its many years of faithful service.

"I found it, Buck!" Ladybird reports. "In 1945, the NAS was known as Naval *Auxiliary* Air Station Oceana; that lasted until 1953 when it became NAS Oceana. It started out as a three hundred and twenty-nine acre facility in 1940, and then slowly expanded until it reached its present size."

"Look at that, Gramps!" The teen 'drives' slowly but surely up to a building on Second Street South, and 'parks' the *System* well within sight of the front of the structure.

It is the home of the St. Petersburg *Sunshine-Herald.* There, emblazoned across a huge metal billboard, is an enormous clock and calendar.

By what this modern family is accustomed to, the timekeeper is ancient. It isn't quite a sundial, but it certainly is august.

It is an aged and obsolete clock by today's standards, with an analog display that shows the time with huge and elongated mechanical hands.

However, of even greater interest is the calendar portion. Although incapable of speech, it seems to be screaming at the family, "February 21, 1945."

At last, there it is, independent confirmation.

A totally uninterested party verifies beyond a doubt that the group has been able to travel backward in time, seventy years to World-War-II-era 1945.

So, regardless of the time adjustments the group has made on the way back to St. Pete's, the newspaper's calendar still makes the statement that they are on the same page, date wise.

Irrespective of the display on the clock-calendar at the *Sunshine-Herald* Building, or what time it is on Iwo Jima; according to the clock on the wall, it is actually 7:00 p.m.

And, right on time, the carport door opens and Dad's voice calls up to the family room for help with the bags from the taxi.

####

2 "Harrison Connor, Cleveland, Ohio"

Lyndsey, Buck, and Ladybird Richardson sit silently meditating over disquieting thoughts concerning the horrendous death toll occasioned to USS *Saratoga*.

James heads downstairs to help the adults with their suitcases. It is brief moments after 7:00 p.m.

Now that the folks are home, Lyndsey realizes that the Iwo Jima scenario will become vital to James' explanation to their parents.

So, the girl picks up the remote control and smoothly 'drives' back to the Japanese island, allowing the *System* to come to rest with the island's coast sitting in the midst of the screen of the HDTV.

Now all is ready for the anticipated arrival of her parents in the rec room, and her opportunity to render support to the argument DJ must be developing in his mind.

Under normal circumstances, Deej would take the stairs two at a time, but this occasion is different. He is pensive as he walks step-by-step down to the carport.

"How in the world can I explain what's happened?" he moans inwardly. "It wasn't my fault; I sure hope they're not mad at me for getting the sofa smashed."

"Hey, what's up, pal?" Dad quickly notes that the boy is in a thoughtful mood.

DJ helps his dad retrieve the cases from the taxi driver, and carry them into the house.

"Dad." James has to lick his lips to moisten them because of his nervousness. "Dad, there's nothing to worry about, but something incredible has happened with the new TV."

"Don't tell me you've wrecked my new TV, James."

Russell James Richardson works long hours at the family business as a transportation consultant.

He has fallen deeply in love with what everybody knows is his new toy, purchased with the fruits of his labors after months of waiting.

The 70-inch large-screen, flat-panel, plasma HDTV is a great way to catch up on things at the end of a hard day at the office, which bureau happens to be just down the hall in their home.

To hear that his baby has been damaged, or even destroyed; the thought beggars description.

He can already feel his hands beginning to tighten around somebody's neck.

"Who broke the TV?" demands Dianne Richardson, coming in on the tail end of the conversation between father and son.

"Nobody broke the TV, Mom, the set's fine. It's what came on it a while ago that's what is wrong."

"What on earth are you talking about, James?"

"Dad, you and Mom have to go and see it for yourselves, because you won't believe it if I just tell you what happened to Lynz and me a little while ago.

"*A World War Two marine on Iwo Jima came through the TV, and just absolutely shot our sofa to pieces with a huge rifle!*"

"What? ... Are you nuts? ... What are you saying?"

"Go upstairs and *see* what happened!"

The invite is totally unnecessary; Russell Richardson is already partway up the stairs with Dianne almost flying, as she places a close second.

"Lyndsey, what have you and your brother been up to? … Dad! Mom! What are you doing here?"

Then his eyes fall on the shattered sofa. He speechlessly points it out to his wife of seventeen years.

"All right! Any one of you; let's have it!" the young mother demands. "Who did that to the sofa? What do you know about this, Buck, Ladybird?"

"Dad, I told you and Mom downstairs that something very unusual has happened with the new TV. You need to look at what Lynz is able to do with the remote control," James recommends.

Buckminster puts in his two-cents worth, "Son, what DJ is telling you is for real. Maybe you and Dianne should sit down, because you're both in for an incredible surprise."

"This is what James stumbled over this afternoon," Lyndsey begins.

"If Lynz can find that marine again, it'll show you how the sofa got wrecked," Deej adds, and, while inwardly cringing, he thinks to himself, "I hope."

Then to Lynz, "Can you take a crack at going back to where we found Bartlett James and took him over to the rock, and then follow him back to the time when he came to apologize to us?"

"I'll try." On the remote, Lyndsey engages the ▲COMPASS until the Pacific island fills the entire viewing area.

The girl recalls that the initial contacts with Bartlett James were made at a distance of about one mile from the volcanic Mount Suribachi at the far end of the island.

She works her way south toward the high ground. Lynz even tries moving backward and forward in time to try locating the young combatant.

Many thousands of marines are on Iwo Jima, but in battle fatigues, they all look alike; this assignment might literally be just as difficult as finding a needle in a haystack.

Naturally, her parents are beginning this experience at a high level of vexation.

Both are entertaining the thought that it is totally, 100 percent, nonsensical that the TV will display what she directs it to show.

But, at the outset, with the strange phenomenon unfolding before their eyes, they must grudgingly acknowledge that the portal is undeniably real.

"TVs aren't supposed to do this," one mumbles.

"James," Russell queries, "are you able to record this onto a DVD?"

"Thanks for asking, Dad," the boy responds. "I started doing that as soon as the marine ended his first visit to the house."

The annoyance, with which they watch initially, changes. First to growing interest, then awe, and finally they are completely spellbound.

Their daughter is exhibiting great skill in maneuvering the remote control, which is exactly the same way she and her sibling had done earlier.

The teen is cautious to ensure she presses only buttons they have used previously, even brief presses on time shift controls.

All are buttons that, she believes and hopes, will cause the HDTV to give the response she needs it to, in order to show their parents the incredible events of a short time before.

Lyndsey negotiates carefully, then, finally, in desperation, pulls up just short of the back of a lone marine.

"Excuse me, sir," she quietly, yet politely calls out to him.

No point in startling him; but in vain.

The response is instant, immediate, and startling. The marine turns rapidly on his heel and, without a moment's hesitation, his M1 carbine jabs into the *System*.

Once again, the Richardson household is intruded upon by the biting end of a piece of military hardware. Four inches of steel barrel penetrate the rec room's airspace.

"Vindication!" The word springs into the minds of both youngsters without the need to search for a suitable thought to express their joint relief.

"Who the (expletive) are you people? … You're civilians! … What do you think you're doing here? … This is a war zone! … Don't you know you could get yourselves killed here? … Hey, what on earth happened to your sofa?"

"I'm sorry to trouble you, sir. It is about our loveseat being wrecked that brings us here.

"One of your marine privates, Bartlett James, accidentally shot up our chesterfield a couple of hours ago.

"We wanted to find him to see if he can try to get us some sort of compensation for the damage. Do you know where we might look for him?"

The young marine officer shrugs his shoulders and says, "Bartlett James? ... Miss, I'm not sure I'll be able to help you with that question ... There are thousands of our guys here, but I can't say I ever heard of anyone with that name."

He gestures with his carbine in the direction of the black-sand beach, presuming that they had arrived on a landing craft of some sort, and says, "You folks better get out of here, while you're still in one piece."

"Could I trouble you, before we go, sir? Could you please tell us the time?" she inquires.

"It's five minutes after three p.m.," the officer responds, checking his watch.

"Is it still February 21, 1945?" she follows up.

"It is. Why do you need to know this?" he quizzes.

"I'm trying to keep a record of the conversations I have had concerning the damaged love seat."

"Thanks for your help," the girl says, and quickly adds, "Sir, may I know your name?"

"Marine Lieutenant Harrison Connor, Cleveland, Ohio, ma'am," he states. "Sorry about your chair, folks."

With that, the .30-caliber carbine and its bearer withdraw from the HDTV.

Once again, the back of Harrison Connor is all that is visible of the officer, now diminishing in size as he returns to his official duties.

Three mouths hang open at this turn of events. 1. Russell's, 2. Dianne's, and, 3. Ladybuck's.

No one from this trio has ever seen anything like this, or even dreamed that such an incident could or would occur in their lifetime.

Even Ladybuck, who earlier witnessed the events surrounding the attack on USS *Saratoga*, is stunned by this most recent experience.

Lyndsey, just to be on the safe side, slowly withdraws from the scene of this latest confrontation with U.S. forces from so many years ago.

"Lynz, could you show Mom and Dad the action with the fleet offshore?"

David James wants all four older family members to have the same quality of information, so that any decisions can be taken with full knowledge of the facts.

Lyndsey, now knowing that it is shortly after 3:05 p.m. on the day of the Japanese mission against the flattop, has in mind that the events surrounding the vicious attack on USS *Saratoga* occurred just before dark.

So, after moving the view to the offshore fleet of ships, she moves ahead in time so that the time-lapse-photography effect can be experienced by the recently arrived parents.

For added verification, she runs backward and then forward, so that they again get the message that, timewise, she has complete control over the view that appears through the screen.

As the light of day begins to fade, the six *kamikaze* aircraft once again begin their inexorable dive onto the deck of the carrier.

As always, five find success, while the remaining one finds only a cold Pacific grave at the hands of the defensive fire of the picket vessels.

Russell, Dianne, and Ladybird are again moved to speechlessness.

How can this spectacle possibly be explicated in any way that will rationally fill in all the gaps, or sort out the pieces of this never-before-seen jigsaw puzzle?

To the kids and their gramps, of course, this is all old hat.

"How is it that we are able to see these things happening on our TV?" Russell asks.

"Grandma had a good way to explain it, Dad," DJ says. "She compared it to something we can easily understand."

"Russell," Ladybird continues, "it seems to me that this is just like looking through a window. What we think we can see on the HDTV is real, and live. So, what is actually happening is that we're seeing it through the television!"

Nonetheless, it is *mission accomplished*, for James and Lyndsey.

Now, all four of the senior family members have to agree, this is no history program, with vintage WWII footage. This is *the real McCoy*.

As Ladybird speaks, Lynz 'chauffeurs' the family back to a view of the entire fleet at Iwo.

Upon arrival, she 'backs up' timewise, so that the scene is fully lit by prevailing sunlight.

#

A string of .30-caliber bullets in the daybed; three visits from Pvt. Bartlett James; in addition to one from Harrison Connor, plus spectacular identical attacks on USS *Saratoga*.

All positively live; all very real; all absolutely genuine. No question. Not in the light of this latest demonstration.

The quandary naturally arises, verbalized by Russell, "What on earth happens now?"

Each member of the group looks at the other individuals and shrugs, as if to say, "I don't have a clue."

Russell decides to break the ice. "What do you kids think you should do with the *System*?"

Lyndsey has a logical thought and expresses it without hesitating, "Well, it's DJ's project. I only entered the equation when Bartlett James' rifle showed up in the rec room for the second time. I vote that this is DJ's call."

Silence fills the room for a few moments, and then, after a quick conference with his wife, Buck speaks, as if for all present, by saying, "That would be fine with Ladybuck and me.

"Frankly, the principle of finders-keepers probably doesn't work in cases like this, but I can't think of another way to settle it."

"Dad, Mom, to be honest," DJ confesses, "I'm still completely puzzled as to what has happened to cause this."

But, now with maturity that is way beyond his years, "Although we all find this phenomenon difficult to understand, I guess we have to accept the fact that it is real.

"What's bothering me the most is why, or better yet, why it's happening at our house, or to us."

"That's a good question, DJ," Russell commends, "but in the meantime, what do you want to do with it?"

"I'm not sure I would want to take this on by myself. Just because Bartlett James fired his rifle at yours truly, that doesn't make me king of the hill.

"I'd like to take your suggestion under advisement and give it a little thought.

"It may be that a situation of this nature would be better addressed if we acted as a committee of sorts.

"We have to make sure that what we do is well thought out, and that at least a majority of the committee thinks that what we're doing is the right thing.

"What do you think I should do?"

"Well, son, try it out for a day or two and see if you still feel the same way on Tuesday or Wednesday; then perhaps we can talk about it again. OK?

"For now, then, you're the straw boss!"

Buck volunteers, "Don't forget that you still need to conduct tests to find out how to use the *System* properly." He explains the experiments that had been conducted just before Russ and Dianne arrived home.

Deej's first decision, in the light of his new temporary responsibility, is almost a no-brainer, "OK. That's pretty much a given. We'll certainly have to keep on experimenting. Then, what else?"

Lyndsey has a mini brainwave, "Deej, maybe it would be a good idea to run your tests around the St. Pete's area, just to make sure that you're thoroughly familiar with it, and aware of what all the buttons on the touch-pad do.

"At least that way you won't go running off into another war zone and getting yourself blasted!"

"Good. Thanks for that, Lynz, and for thinking of me. Any other suggestions?" the young boy asks.

In the absence of a reply, DJ says, "One thing we must all agree on. That is to keep word of this inside our family, and I sure hope you can see the wisdom of this.

"I have a powerful feeling that the awesome capabilities we have seen today would be of extreme interest to any bad guys out there, and we'll have to be very careful who finds out about it."

"No argument there, James," Ladybird offers on behalf of the listening quintet.

"Lynz's suggestion is good. So if any of you would like to be part of the experimentation phase, you'll be very welcome to have a full share in it."

Deej, again, "I guess if we're all going to have a part in the testing, it will be a mistake to leave anyone out. We'll need to involve all of us right from the start.

"Perhaps we'll get under way with the ones who have top seniority here.

"Grandma, would you like to be first? Gramps can help if you need it."

"DJ, I have an idea on something that might help us. Do you mind if I try a little experiment first?" Russell asks his son.

"Go ahead, Dad."

"Mom," said Russell, addressing his own mother, the 'driver,' "before we move on, would you try a little test for us?

"This might be not only interesting, but might save us a lot of time and work. Would you take a crack at pressing some number buttons?

"What can we try first? ... Maybe try the numbers for a date a few years ago, say, '2-0-0-8.' I guess anything but this year, and see what happens. The *System* is in '1945' mode at the moment."

"Hold on, there, Grandma. I'll be the note-taker while you're 'driving,'" DJ says.

"All right, '2-0-0-8' ... Wait ... Nothing ... "

Buck suggests, "Try waiting for ten or twelve seconds."

"OK. I've waited ten, twelve, fifteen seconds more, and still nothing!"

"Just a second ... There's an ENTER button; let me try using it. '2-0-0-8' and ENTER."

"Bingo!"

"What's happening, Lynz? I'm trying to write this down," as Deej struggles to see the TV.

"DJ, we were looking just now at the 1945 battlefield on Iwo Jima," she responds, "and suddenly it changes to a lush green tropical paradise. It's as if we instantly traveled through a lot of years to a date in the past or future, either before the fighting started or after ... well, I guess it's most likely after it finished."

"There's someone over there," DJ volunteers. "Can you 'drive' over and take a look? ... It's a gardener; over on the right side of the scene ... He's working on the landscaping. Can we ask him the date? Anyone speak Japanese? … I guess not."

Ladybuck easily and smoothly clears most of the distance, leaving ten or so meters between the family's position and that of the landscaper.

Although the man is clearly in their field of view, he seems oblivious to their presence.

Ladybird adds, "I still can't believe this is happening."

No sooner are those words out of his grandmother's mouth, when to everyone's wonderment and surprise, DJ puts the corporate notepad down, and then does something truly spectacular.

Dianne, unaware of James' intentions, leans over, picks up the discarded book, and prepares to keep track of activities while James is otherwise occupied.

Apprehensively, yet with growing confidence, the young teen walks up close to the big HD plasma device. He wants to perform an experiment of his own. He removes his wristwatch as he walks.

He thrusts his right hand into the screen, just as a test. Wonder of wonders, the screen permits his hand to enter up to his elbow. Yet it remains intact; it fails to break. His hand is not harmed.

"I had an idea that might happen," the teen says.

Next, withdrawing his hand from the screen, he replaces it with his right foot. Again no breakage, and no damage to the boy.

Then, David James Richardson steps out of the rec room of his family's home in St. Petersburg, Florida, USA, onto the manicured lawn of that faraway island, apparently in the year 2008.

For the first time in the history of mankind, a human being has traveled at the speed of light from the United States of America to the island of Iwo Jima, Prefecture of Tokyo, Japan.

Albert Einstein is nowhere in sight (having died in 1955), but he surely would be happy to know that he was right on the nose with respect to time travel.

Within the confines of the house, not a single word is spoken.

If one can be conjured up, what will it be? Incredible? Dumbfounding? Stupendous? Astonishing? Unbelievable? …

It won't suffice ... Whatever adjective is chosen ... The remaining five Richardsons will find each one of these words to be true, but no single word can express the amazement that takes the breath of each individual member of the family.

Deej walks the remaining fifteen or so paces over to the oriental gardener, bows, reaches out and shakes his hand; then, bows again. James taps his wrist to indicate to the aged landscaper that he wishes to know the time.

The older man shows DJ his wristwatch, and James signals to the house with one finger, two fingers and zero, zero (twelve o'clock noon).

The teen salutes the elder in thanks, turns around and walks back to the *System*.

The Japanese man, slightly puzzled, follows the lad with his eyes, but says nothing.

Ducking down, the family's hero-of-the-hour coolly steps onto the wood floor of the Richardson's home.

Russell, Dianne, Buck, Ladybuck, and LP stand (or sit) in utter amazement, but not in silence.

"How did you do that?"

"Why did you do that?"

"You could have been killed!"

"You could have wrecked my TV!"

"TVs aren't supposed to act that way."

"Well, it seems logical that if two marines could stick huge rifles out of our TV, and start trying to blast me, then I should be able to do the same thing, except in reverse," says DJ.

"The gardener's watch says twelve noon, January 1; there was no year on the display."

"What was it like on the other side, James?" Lyndsey inquires, although she receives no answer.

Russell, "This is fantastic! ... What in the world have you found here, Deej?"

"Good grief!" Myriads of thoughts flood Russell's mind as he tries to get his grey matter around the whole scenario.

All this, in addition to what he has seen by way of the HD screen—to say nothing of DJ's shenanigans—is really messing with the man's head.

The whole idea of his son being able to enter into that paradisaic world through a television set, without immediate harm or apparent danger is fascinating to him.

"DJ, could you do that again?"

James, now oozing with confidence, digital camera in hand, steps out of the family room, through the *System*, and onto the same lawn next to what was formerly the shell-pocked, black-sand beach of a tiny island called Iwo Jima.

Once more DJ strolls over to the aging oriental. He bows again, shows the gardener his camera, points to it with his free hand; the gent nods, and James composes his picture using the camera's viewing screen and takes a digital photograph of the humble worker.

He finishes by panning around the scene, taking a few seconds of video, then stows the camera in his shirtfront pocket. He bows again to his new friend and after an about-face, walks the short distance back to where the *System* stands waiting.

From Iwo, he hands the digital camera from his shirt pocket to his mother, who accepts it with stunned surprise.

During all this activity, his paternal grandmother is required to maneuver the remote control to keep the family in a position where each one can see whenever James moves during his royal walkabout.

With notes and James' camera in hand, Dianne watches as her son calmly disembarks from the electronic portal, and onto the engineered wood floor of the family home.

Just like a modern-day movie hero, not a hair of his head has been disturbed. In fact, mirroring a feature of a certain make-believe Secret Intelligence Service (formerly MI6) agent, he's not even breathing heavily.

The young mother's fascination with the recent events is heightened, while her earlier apprehension and concern are reawakened, as her teenaged son takes the camera from her hand.

He displays the mini-screen on the back, so that she can see the picture he has just taken on that tiny island that looks as if it could easily be mistaken for a miniature version of the Garden of Eden.

"Hey, if that actually works the way it seems, it means DJ just traveled all the way to that Japanese island, right back to St. Pete's in a single second each way! That is ... !

"How could he possibly do that? ... Unimaginable! ... You know what? We still have to confirm the year of what we're looking at. No one here is able to speak Japanese, so we can't ask the gardener."

In the time it has taken him to climb from one world to the other, in that "single second," DJ has traveled 7,730 miles each way.

That truly meets the specifications to be called "one small step for man; one giant leap for mankind."

Lyndsey, "Deej, would it be OK if you let Mom try to bring it home to St. Pete's and go to the *Sunshine-Herald* office and check out the display on the front of the building there? What do you think?"

"Could Grandpa bring it home? He's been watching you guys do it for long enough to have memorized the procedures," Dianne queries.

"Give it a try, Grandpa Buck."

"Thanks, guys. This is awesome. Since we're sitting together, perhaps Ladybird could keep track of the note-taking."

Ladybird was agreeable to the latter suggestion.

Russell, "That would be a good move, because it will give us the year in St. Pete's, at least.

"From that we could extrapolate the time from PIE over to Universal Coordinated Time (UCT).

"Then we can add the difference between UCT and IWO to the result of our first calculation to verify the destination time (that is in effect at the site we've been viewing. In this case, that will be IWO)."

"DJ, do we need to keep track of how long it takes us to 'drive' home to St. Pete's? We can add the difference to find out the date and time of your space walk on Iwo."

"That's a fair thought, Dad, but no need. The thing is that, timewise, the trip from IWO over to PIE, St. Pete's, is very short and not worth including in our calculations.

"You'll be able to see how little time it takes after we make the trip.

"I guess we'll also have to take the International Date Line into account as well."

"Daylight saving time, too!" Ladybuck pipes in.

Dianne, "Yuck!"

Buck adds, "Come to think of it, if you visit any continent other than the Americas, and need daylight to be able to see when you get there, then I guess you'll have to travel when it's nighttime here in Florida."

"When we had to move around a bit earlier, we found a way to avoid that, by changing time slots before leaving for a particular destination," Lyndsey reminds her folks.

"Just move back a few hours until we have the daylight we need, if that's feasible. Of course, that may not always be possible, due to the particular circumstances when we get there, or any urgency issues," she proposes.

James, "You're right! … OK, folks, let's head back to our home base, and we'll check out the newspaper as you suggest and set ourselves straight.

"Grandpa Buck, here's what we need you to do."

DJ is glad to be able to get his grandparents involved. It is a good opportunity to share this newfound excitement with everyone in the family.

At the same time, he thinks that it would be even better if the Grovers, his mom's family, could be involved too. But that will have to come at a later point in time.

"We're facing roughly south right now. See if you can re-orient the *System* so that it's pointing in a northeasterly direction.

"Then travel over the Pacific Ocean towards Hawaii. It doesn't really matter whether you hit North or South America," says the straight-A Geog. student to his grandfather.

"Once we hit the west coast of either continent, and we identify it, you can turn in the direction of Los Angeles; we can use that as our arrival port, and then turn east.

"All right, Gramps! Let's rock and roll."

The 58-year-old baby boomer smoothly rotates the group from right to left, using the ◀COMPASS button, until he figures, at a guess, that he has turned roughly 110°, away from the island.

Now, before he stands heavily on the 'gas,' he first holds down the ▲VOL key until he is three thousand feet or so in the air and has a clear view for several dozen miles.

Now he operates the 'gas pedal' by depressing the ▲COMPASS key and holding it down. He feels quite comfortable in the driver's seat; on the busted sofa, that is.

First Fiji, and then the Hawaiian Islands begin to drift by on their port side, the latter in increasing darkness as nightfall closes in.

"I would rather 'drive' in daylight. Is there some way we could go about moving forward or back a few hours in time."

"Pull in to the Aloha Tower at Honolulu Harbor. You can use its clock to adjust your time," Ladybird suggests. "Then you'll have an exact moment to refer to."

Buck steers north, easily locating Oahu and the large commercial harbor used by both freighters and cruise ships.

The clock faces are displayed on each surface of a four-sided tower and readily provide the assistance Buck needs to adjust his time a full fourteen hours forward.

"That's true, Grandma Ladybuck. Thanks for the suggestion," James responds.

Their last time check had been the island gardener's watch, which had indicated twelve o'clock noon, which translates into 6:00 p.m. the previous day at Honolulu, given the time difference and the International Date Line.

"Don't forget, Granddad," he continues as Buck makes his adjustment to the Hawaiian clock, "we need to confirm the watch time I got on Iwo, which we can actually do looking at this HNL timepiece.

"But we also need to verify what *year* this is, so that we know how far we have traveled in time. The *Sunshine-Herald* display in St. Pete's will tell us the exact date, so that we can figure out the information for Iwo Jima.

"We need to be sure that the '2-0-0-8 and ENTER' really did take us to the year 2008."

Once more full daylight prevails as Buckminster takes the *System* out of the Honolulu location, except that he is on a westward vector.

The portal crosses over the short distance between the Tower and the huge U.S. naval facility at Pearl Harbor.

Buck smoothly drops down, pausing briefly at the gleaming white memorial to BB-39 USS *Arizona*.

The over to the adjacent museum ship BB-63 USS *Missouri*.

These two ships are considered the sites of the beginning and end of the Pacific phase of the Second World War.

Buck next eases the view off to the east, and heads out past Diamond Head in what he guesses is the general direction of Los Angeles on the U.S. mainland.

A very brief time later, they arrive over the mass of what appears to be a long peninsular of land, which resembles Florida, but cannot be the Sunshine State. It is on the wrong side of North America.

Lyndsey, "Baja … Baja California!"

"You've got it, Lynz. Good for you!"

"Grandpa Buck! Go north to Los Angeles; then turn east again. Don't go too fast; it doesn't take long."

So he makes a left at Baja, and then a right at Los Angeles.

This time, the freeways are loaded with cars, giving a clear indication that the family is making this trip on relatively current time. Buck makes the required 90° turns.

There is no requirement to find lower-lying land, or passes through the Rocky Mountains. To avoid banging into the Rockies, Buck elevates the group to clear the very highest peaks, adding but a split second to the trip.

Rapidly traversing the United States toward the east coast, Buckminster turns at Virginia Beach, this time allowing a not-so-brief respite in sight of Runway 05R at Oceana Naval Air Station, to visit with the F-22 Raptors.

The family is on a timeline probably in the year 2008, when Oceana is alive and well in its latest configuration. So, the usual "ooohs" and "aaahs" from the male contingent.

Then he 'flies' off to Jacksonville, where they turn toward their home and cross the hinterland of Florida without incident.

Past Orlando and its well-known theme park; across the Bay, overflying MacDill Air Force Base.

Across the now extant Pier toward 2nd Street South to within sight of the newspaper's building where the digital calendar mounted on the edifice shows: Tuesday, January 1, 2008.

So, in just a few minutes, including their stops at the Aloha Tower and Pearl Harbor, without setting foot outside his son's home,

Buckminster Richardson has broken all known speed records, even that for the SR-71 Blackbird.

"Alright; that's better. This is a much more user-friendly view," the old-timer allows.

#

"Guys, there may be something we can try here, since we have just made a trip in time; but we'll need to make a careful note of this.

"Gramps, do you have a button on the remote marked BACK, or LAST, or RETURN?"

"DJ, there's one here marked CANCEL. The only other one that might fit is one that is shaped like a triangle with no markings on it." ['▲' - The 'DELTA' or triangle is the international symbol for 'change.']

"OK, can you push that DELTA button? Just one quick press and let's see what happens.

"Nothing happened. Do you have another button you can try it with, Grandpa Buck?" the boy asks

"I don't like to choose all by myself. I don't want to louse the portal up for you," Buckminster replies.

"Gramps, you're the one who wanted to experiment previously. What was it you said? 'Every button so far has had a logical effect tied to it.'

"OK. Let's see. What's that blue button next to the DELTA? Try that, and if it doesn't work try the 'Cancel' button beside it."

"Both buttons together, but nothing again, Deej. Sorry. I'm trying DELTA with the 'Cancel' button now. Nothing again."

"OK, try the MUTE button with the DELTA. That 'change' key has to do something related to moving the *System* around."

Buckminster, "'Mute' and then DELTA."

"Nothing!"

"OK. Try the rocker switch that is marked 'Page,' and then the DELTA."

"'Page +,' or 'Page –'?" the ancient one inquires.

"Start with the 'Page plus,' and DELTA.

"Grandma Ladybuck, are you getting all this?"

"Yes, DJ. So far, so good," Buckminster's wife replies.

"'Page plus' and DELTA … Nothing, again."

"Do it again, just for the sake of trying," the disappointment is to be heard in his voice.

"One more time, DELTA and 'Page plus' … Still nothing. Shall I try it again?"

"No. Try the 'Page minus.'"

"DELTA and 'Page minus' ... Hey! That worked. Hold on ... What's happened? ... We've gone from the *Sunshine-Herald* on January 1, 2008, back to the Aloha Tower."

The excitement instantly registers in James' voice.

"Try the same combination of buttons, Gramps!" the thrilled boy calls. "Keep going, except slowly," he directs.

At the next DELTA key-press, the view switches over to the ancient gardener on the embattled island of Iwo Jima.

In response to another stab at the combined buttons, the scene reverts to a view of most of the U.S. fleet off the Japanese island.

A fourth DELTA brings them to the 5:00 p.m. timeslot on February 21, 1945, and the family once more gets to view the *kamikaze* attack on USS *Saratoga*.

"Stop there, Gramps," James instructs. "We have to think about this for a second or two."

"What's happening here?" Russell asks, in bewilderment. "What makes the *System* decide to pick out these locations to make stops?"

Ladybird is often the person with the answers to difficult question for the family, and this occasion is no different. "Can you have Buckminster try something, Deej?" she asks. "I think what's happening here, is that we are running backward through the recent time changes we have made to the *System*."

"We started out just a minute or so ago, at the newspaper's office, and the clock display showed Tuesday, January 1, 2008.

"Then, in response to the 'Page minus' along with the DELTA key, we moved to our previous location where we made a time shift, which was the Aloha Tower.

"Then we did a DELTA over to the old gentleman doing the landscaping.

"After sighting the gardener, we wound up off the coast where we could see the 1945 fleet at dusk.

"That's because Lyndsey changed time slots just there because night was falling on the fleet and it was getting too dark to see any longer.

"Finally, we went back to USS *Saratoga* again, which was the time shift prior to that.

"So what's happening is that we are time-shifting along the stream of changes that we've made to the *System*.

"Can you get Buckminster to try using the DELTA, but with 'page plus' this time, to see if it runs back up those same changes that we just viewed?"

Ladybuck's thinking is that the 'plus' and 'minus' buttons might simply be a means of reversing the DELTA action.

"OK, Gramps, there are your orders. Try it slowly, though, and, stop if the wrong scene shows up, because we'll have to think about what might have changed to cause that."

Buck carefully presses the DELTA and 'Page plus' buttons just once and pauses to allow the family to view the result, then continues.

"Right again, Grandma," James congratulates, as the view reverts from USS *Sara* in distress over to a daylight view of the entire fleet prior to the Japanese attack on the flattop. Here is where Lynz had gone in search of increased daylight. Next, quite correctly, the picture then changes to the Japanese landscaper once again.

At the next press on DELTA and 'Page plus,' our scene changes back to the Honolulu Tower.

"Why are we seeing only certain views?" DJ asks. "Why do we not see the *Sunshine-Herald*'s clock? That is a stop that we made recently," he questions.

"Remember, Deej," his sister clarifies. "Can I explain this, Grandma Ladybuck? I think I've got it sorted out, from what you said before.

"When Grandpa Buck 'flew' us back to the newspaper, we only 'arrived,' so to speak. There was no time shift involved while we were there.

"So that means that the DELTA 'Page +' and 'Page -' buttons will not take us to locations; they will only take us to whatever scene we were viewing when a time change was made.

"The newspaper's clock doesn't show up because we 'drove' to this location, and that didn't trigger a stop that DELTA would recognize."

"That's right, Lyndsey, you've got it. So, I've noted that down just for future reference."

"Grandma," James inquires, "Do you have all of those time slot moves marked down."

"I do, but, because it's going to be tricky remembering exactly where we made changes to our precise spot in the stream of time.

"I started a while ago, writing down each time shift we make, including the date and time of departure, if we know it, as well as the location being displayed when the time shift began.

"As well, I've begun recording whether or not we'll be able to DELTA our way *back* to that location. Anyone taking notes will have to keep in mind the need always to mark those things down."

James responds, "That should work out well for everyone.

"Grandma, thanks.

"Perhaps we'll be able to use the DELTA key to shift back to places we have recently visited, like going back to the newspaper's office, for example.

"It could easily be faster than 'driving' from location to location."

"So did everyone catch that?" James now questions. "The DELTA button combined with the 'Page minus' key switches us from the present view back to our last time shift at the location at which that change took place.

"It apparently can be used continuously to move back down the changes we have made. I have avoided going back too far, because we might run into Bart James at the time of his first visit.

"The DELTA and 'Page plus' keys can be used to reverse those same movements, one step at a time.

"I guess we should understand, too, that the reason the DELTA and 'Page *plus*' keys didn't work at first was because, at that moment, there was nowhere to go.

"We first have to go backward along our chain of changes before we can tell it to move us forward again."

The teen is ecstatic that, at last, the family has discovered a faster way of moving up and down in the stream of time, if only to the past time shifts.

"OK. I think that synopsis James gave us fits in with my evidence," the matriarch commended.

"Meanwhile, the clock on the wall says it's time for Buckminster and me to quit and get out of here for the night."

The clock shows that it is 11:15 p.m. and all can read the home calendar that shows the date to be Saturday, February 21, 2015, so they ignore what the newspaper's clock display says.

After agreeing to leave the *System* facing the journal's office until morning, the meeting adjourns for the night.

The motion carries unanimously without being proposed, seconded, or a vote being taken.

####

3 Ernie Pyle on Ie Shima

The clock on the family room wall says that it is 8:30 a.m. The calendar beside it shows the current date to be Sunday, February 22, 2015. Buck and Ladybuck Richardson have not yet arrived for the first day of experimentation activities.

"So, DJ, while we're waiting for your granddad and grandma to get here, tell us what you already know and then you can figure out where to go from there."

"Dad, according to yesterday's notes, the major player buttons are pretty much worked out.

"The forward, reverse, and both sides COMPASS buttons cause horizontal direction movements; forward, backward, left, and right.

"The up and down VOL buttons raise, or lower the *System*, respectively.

"The forward and backward CH buttons move us through time.

"Holding any one of those eight buttons down causes the action to take place at high speed, which is what were using yesterday, to go to and from the Japanese island.

"From last night, we know how to use the DELTA and 'Page minus' to back up through our recent time shifts, and DELTA + 'Page plus' to return by steps to our current position.

"Could you get Grandma to do the keystroke recording for us again, when she gets here, Dad, and then we can let Mom 'drive'? I can do the writing in the meantime, but I'll just list new buttons; ones we haven't used before, except for the time travel moves."

"Your show, Deej," his dad says. "We can do anything you like ... I had been wondering about whether we really needed to keep marking down every keystroke. That's probably a good move."

"You know, Dad, something occurs to me. Would you guys always remind our 'chauffeur,' before we ever go anywhere, to first 'drive' over to the newspaper's offices, and double-check the date and time that the *System* thinks it is?

"Until we get used to the *System*, forgetting to do that might get us confused or even lost someplace. I guess we're yet to discover whether that's possible or not."

"OK, Mom. Go slowly, and don't press anything without first letting us know exactly which buttons you're using. Be deliberate. Try hard not to press two buttons at a time. That might make us lose our bearings, and perhaps that would leave us unable to figure out what has happened at some later point.

"If you run into something you don't like the look of, be ready to reverse out of it right away! If you're not sure, just ask Lynz or me. It's better to be safe than sorry."

#

When the doorbell rings, Russell remembers immediately who is expected, and says, "Hold it, guys; that'll be Grandpa Buck and Ladybuck ... Back in a flash!"

#

"Hey, everybody! Good after-nine, people," Buck chirps, as the house clock ticks over 8:40 a.m.

"Hi Grandma! Hi Gramps! We're just getting started. Mom's 'driving' and DJ's making the notes for now.

"I think Dad wants you to keep records instead of Deej, Grandma, if you wouldn't mind." Lyndsey updates the patriarch and matriarch of Russell's side of the family.

"I'd love to. Thanks," Ladybird says. "Anything," she adds, "just don't ask me to climb through the TV in my skirt!"

After the laughter dies down, "By the way, Grandma, DJ says there is no need to record keystrokes when they are just horizontal directions, or up and down. He thinks it would be good if we tracked those we use when we're traveling in time.

"Otherwise, just the ones that are new, or when we're doing the number thing, and selecting a specific year to travel to. Too, when we're using the DELTA key, as you said last night."

"OK! That'll make things easier for you, Bird," Buckminster comments, using his own pet name for his wife.

"Grandma, since you're the keeper of the notes, DJ has asked us to always remind whoever's 'driving,' to first take us over to the newspaper office, and double-check the date and time; so that we don't get lost somewhere."

"That's a good idea! I'll keep that in mind. Thanks, Lyndsey."

#

"Say, how did you guys sleep last night?" Ladybird questions.

"Worst night's sleep I've had in a long time, Mom," Russell replies. "Dianne and I barely slept a wink. A bit too much excitement, I guess."

Dianne says, "I just couldn't get the image out of my mind of DJ gallivanting all over the place on that island."

"That bothered us a lot, too," Ladybuck reports. "I never thought I'd ever see the day when someone would step into a television picture, at least, not from the front."

Deej retorts, "Didn't bother me a bit! How about you, Lynz?"

"My head hit the pillow and I was gone; it didn't stop me from sleeping."

#

"OK, LP, you get to choose! For our number one experiment; where in the whole wide world would you like us to take you?"

"Jessica sent me a text late last week. She said she saw a Killdeer plover on the school's playing field on Friday. Can we go and have a look-see?

"It will restrict us to the St. Pete's area, and will give us practice at both physical movement and time travel."

"Holy cow! You're easy to please ... OK, how do you want to do this, Lynz? … Whereabouts on the field do you need us to go?"

"Well, Jess said the plover was halfway between the goalposts and the running track at the east end of the field. I thought that we could set up the *System* to run forward in time from about 8:00 a.m., just until the bird shows up."

"You're the 'driver,' Mom. Go ahead."

It is now 8:51 a.m. Very dutifully, Dianne travels in time to adjust the through-screen display of the *Sunshine-Herald*'s 2008 date and time from last evening's operation (plus any time that has accrued during the overnight period), to match the house calendar and clock.

Following this, the family group now has an immediate requirement to match the journal's calendar to Friday's information for the bird sighting (February 20, 2015), which Dianne does faultlessly. It then takes mere seconds to back up to 8:00 a.m., and then to hightail it over to the goalpost at the east end of the playing field.

Lyndsey feels Jessica was unlikely to have been there any earlier than that hour, so it should make a good starting point. The rest is just a case of waiting while Dianne scans quickly through to around lunchtime, when the plover and Jessica both show up at what they estimate is around 12:30 p.m.

A DELTA to the journal office is not on this occasion going to solve the question as to the exact time of arrival of the bird.

As the folks learned last night, DELTA only brings them back to the moment of their last time-travel move, which, on this occasion, was actually a timeslot change that took place on the school grounds.

It's somewhat like a regular TV. When one changes channels, the program on the first channel will continue to run while they are away watching the second channel. But, if the second channel is a video, and they fast-forward it, the first channel has no knowledge of the fast-forward action.

Similarly, using DELTA to move back in time to the paper will still only display the time at which they last time-skipped at the journal, no updating will have been recorded. Hence, the DELTA button is limited in this way also.

As it is lunchtime at the playing field, several other people are loitering around also.

Not wanting to expose the time portal to her friend, or any of the others, Lyndsey encourages her mother to fast-forward until Jess finishes looking at the bird, and she, along with any onlookers, leaves; thus, the sixteen-year-old prodigy escapes notice.

Jessica's Friday assertion proves to be correct. A Killdeer it is. Lynz, the family's own bird specialist, is the acknowledged expert in this field.

Killdeers allow themselves to be approached quite readily, so Lyndsey takes her digital camera, and performs her own version of James' earlier extra-vehicular activity.

Holding her skirt against her legs just above the knees, she does her best to be as graceful as possible, but she thinks to herself, "This is worse than getting out of an SUV."

Nonetheless, she gracefully steps through the plasma TV's screen, as if disembarking from a minivan, and is happy she is successful.

The high-school senior cautiously walks over to the plover, and after a few words in a very calm voice, to reassure the bird of her good intentions, she takes a digital photograph of the bird.

Fortunately, the killdeer plover allows itself to be approached quite readily, so Lynz's picture is a good close-up.

Having checked the results on the preview screen on the reverse of the camera, she picks her way over to where the portal, barely visible at the best of times, patiently waits.

However, before embarking, she holds up her right hand with index finger raised to the 'driver,' for this operation, Dianne, to say "Just a second."

She walks slowly and thoughtfully around the portal, and then steps from the grass of the high school playing field back into the house.

"Wow," she exclaims, "that's fascinating! James, I asked you yesterday what the *System* looked like from the other side. Well, I just found out for myself. It looks like a clean, round hole that is simply hanging on nothing, and I could just barely make out the five of you inside it."

"While you guys are chatting over that experience, I'll run upstairs and put on a pot of coffee, and switch on the kettle. We can have tea and refreshments."

However, Dianne is not finished 'chauffeuring' for the day. "Come up in about ten minutes and it should be all ready for you."

Everyone seems to agree that this has been an excellent first trial run; and all without leaving the area of St. Pete's.

#

So, here it is, well over a half-hour later, and much refreshed, especially for those who had missed breakfast.

"Mom, this is our second practice run with you 'driving.' Could you take us slowly over to the Pier and back?

"You can try changing height levels as you go; Up to 500 feet or so, and back down again, should be ideal.

"You know, if you do a good job of this, we might allow you to look around to see if there are any dolphins in sight in Tampa Bay.

"So, let's see how you do that, and Grandma Ladybuck can write down any new keystrokes for this trip, too."

Russell to Deej, "Did you want me to remind you to get your mother to 'drive' us over to the *Sunshine-Herald*, and make adjustment to the date and time, DJ?"

"Gosh, Dad! Already I had forgotten."

"Mom, Dad's right; the *System* thinks we're still on last Friday at the school. Could you do that for us, first?"

The initial move is to go back to the newspaper in order to reset the date to February 22, 2015, at 10:35 a.m., which is in agreement with the wall-clock, and the house calendar, and then, 'let's boogie on down!'

Hence, Dianne is in the driver's seat with instructions to go over to the Pier, just for practice, and no point in hurrying, right? Therefore, no rush it is!

The female Generation Xer intends to take the 'scenic route,' and so, first raises the view up a couple of hundred feet, then heads away from the *Herald's* offices.

She points the unit west, toward the on-ramp for Interstate 375, slowly undulating as she goes, varying her altitude between 100 and 600 feet.

As she proceeds with each move, she calls out clearly which of the buttons she is about to use; how she is pressing them, whether once, twice, or more times, or holding them down, which, on a short trip like this, will likely be unnecessary.

This permits her son to choose which items he will get Ladybird to record for their files.

DJ admires the very professional 'driving' style his mother is using.

He notes for the whole group. "I hope you are noticing that Mom is able to direct the *System* forward and at the same time vary the height. So the portal is able to handle the two instructions simultaneously."

Dianne continues the oscillating course above the center lane of Interstate-375 for about one mile, and then turns north to follow I-275 for six miles to State Route 92, which leads the group to the causeway known as Gandy Boulevard.

Gandy includes a section of raised road surface that runs eight or ten feet above the waters of Tampa Bay.

Combined, together, SR 92 and Gandy make a smooth trip of ten miles to South Dale Mabry Highway in the city of Tampa.

A two-mile southbound sector is all that is needed to bring them over MacDill Air Force Base. Finally, a 5-mile over-water run to the Pier in St. Petersburg.

She turns onto the line of 2nd Avenue NE, and 'drives' in the general direction of their home.

Fifty yards west of the Pier, she makes a 180° turn and, proceeding very smoothly, slows the *System* down to a crawl.

As is her custom, she thrills at the beautiful sight of the five stories of the inverted pyramid structure at the end of the causeway that juts out into the bay. Now, the young mother comes to a full stop a little west of the edifice, without any untoward incident, so that the well-known landmark is fully in sight for all present.

Both north and south of the Pier, schools of frisky bottlenose dolphins busily show off.

The shiny creatures repeatedly leap out of Tampa Bay, only to plunge so smoothly back into the warm water.

The family always takes delight in such natural sights; they are so incredibly enjoyable to an appreciative eye.

"That's great, Mom," Deej commends,

"Could you please take us over to Whitted? Just for a look around … for the guys." he begs.

Dianne rotates the view so that it is toward the south, facing the adjacent Albert Whitted Airport.

This is a small airfield where small private aircraft are departing and arriving repeatedly.

Many "ooohs" and "aaahs" are heard from the three musketeers because of this sight. Especially is this so as Dianne closes in on the 'east-west' Runway 06, where most of the action takes place.

However, the cries of delight from the men are accompanied by expressions of boredom from the ladies present.

Dianne has a private thought, "One of these days, I'll take these guys over to Windsor Castle, and check out Queen Mary's old dolls' house. That'll make 'em howl."

#

"Kids, what is the default view for the *System*?" Russell inquires. He enunciates the words carefully; this is a drastic change of subject.

"You know, Dad, we don't have an answer for that yet," DJ responds.

"But even if one doesn't exist, it may be that we should get accustomed to using the *Sunshine-Herald* as if it is our default. We can simply wind up every trip by parking there."

"Stationing ourselves outside the paper," Russell agrees, "would be good. That will often be helpful for us."

Ladybird is the note-taker, "Something else for you to give some thought to during the experiments, is, I guess, watching out for buttons that appear to give no response.

"They probably all produce some reaction, but that change could be so small, that it may not be immediately apparent.

"Too, it may be that some buttons only work in conjunction with others; as we found out in connection with the DELTA key."

"Right, Mom!" Dianne adds, agreeing with her mother-in-law. "That's something DJ is going to have to work on. There are still at least ten keys on the remote that we haven't tried yet.

"Listen, I was going to do us something special for lunch. Can Lyndsey take over the remote for a while? I need to spend a little time on the meal. Is that OK?" Dianne asks.

Deej, "Sure, Mom."

"We're still testing, guys, so, Lynz, if you're OK to 'drive' for a while, can you take us to the newspaper office, just to check and see that our date and time are right on the beam?

"If you find everything is A-OK, then perhaps you could take us back to Iwo Jima."

There is no adjustment to make; the journal's clock and calendar both match the house data, as their prior activities consisted of simply 'cruising' around the area of St. Pete's on real time.

After verifying the date display, Lyndsey 'swings' the *System* over to a westerly vector, and hits 'warp factor one.'

In less than a half-minute the group is over the U.S. west coast, adjusting on the fly to be sure that the line of flight will be south of the islands of Hawaii.

While in flight, the youngster calls out "'1-9-4-5' and ENTER," to allow her grandmother to record the time shift.

Through the screen, there is little difference between the 'before' and 'after' views.

Everything is proceeding smoothly, so far, until, "Ouch! Sorry! I nuked two buttons together! ... I may have hit the extra button twice.

"Oh, no! For a minute, I lost track of what I was trying to do. I may even have held one of them down for a few seconds or even more. I'm just not sure.

"Why do these things always happen to me?" James' sister moans.

#

Ultimately, a sharp pair of eyes spots a small island coming into their view on the edge of what they are able to see through the screen.

"Don't worry for now, Lynz," James encourages. "It doesn't appear to have made any difference anyway.

"We are on the west side of this island, and the sea does look rougher than it was yesterday; and, come to think of it, this island looks smaller."

As she closes in on what she hopes is Iwo Jima the scene of DJ's initial confrontation with Bart J., others in the party spot another, much larger island off to the east of the smaller island.

That had not been in the view they had seen on their earlier foray to Iwo.

Lyndsey spots a small group of men in what looks like a cemetery. She is still in hope of being able to find that same Missouri lad who had destroyed the family's sofa.

Perhaps these men will be able to help her to find him.

Her parents really have no need to be placated any longer. Russell and Dianne appear to be thoroughly convinced, albeit dumbfounded, by the sights the girl had displayed to them the previous evening.

The teenaged 'driver' cautiously moves in on the area of now-devastated ground where she sees the group of men gathered.

They draw in closer, and the Richardson sextet is able to bring its eyesight into focus on the scene.

It again becomes obvious that, like the young marine whose shots had initiated this whole adventure, these young men are dressed in American fatigues from a bygone era.

The dungarees definitely do not have the appearance of twenty-first century U.S. military-issue battle dress.

The helmets the men are wearing, (to protect their heads from flying shrapnel and projectiles,) seem to have a different silhouette to the headgear American soldiers wear today.

Nary a flak jacket or bulletproof vest in sight.

The young prodigy halts the forward motion before the family gets in too close to the soldiers.

Voices can be heard, but not with any clarity. The Richardsons strain with all of their ears, but are unable to discern the words being spoken.

They are infantrymen, gathered around a small wood-plank marker nailed to the top of a one-by-three-inch piece of lumber planted in the ground.

A solitary vintage American army helmet stands on lone sentry duty before the stake; as if to denote that this spot is the final resting place of a fighting man.

The assembly appears solemn, as the men seem to be grieving.

The gathering concludes abruptly, when one man, whose apparel bears the uniform markings of an officer, throws a pouch-like object into what has recently been a cluster of trees and bushes.

Subsequently, the men leave on foot in several directions.

Lyndsey, "Deej, this may not be the same place. These men don't have the same appearance as the boy on Iwo Jima.

"Their uniforms are different. I can't say why, but it might be that they are a different color.

"Maybe that's why you also noticed that this island seemed to be different from the one we visited yesterday."

With the meeting ended, the men gone; and with the sun getting ever higher in the sky, Lyndsey negotiates the *System* in to where the lone marker stands. It bears the crude but simple caption:

AT THIS SPOT
THE 77TH INFANTRY DIVISION
LOST A BUDDY
ERNIE PYLE
18 APRIL 1945

That name strikes a chord! The folksy words are very touching, but that name. It rings a bell with Ladybuck, unlike all the others in the group.

"Ernie Pyle?" she says questioningly. "He's not a soldier … or, at least, he wasn't.

"There was a program on TV yesterday; I watched it while you were at your appointment at the hardware store, Buck.

"Russell, I'm pretty sure they mentioned that gentleman's name, or a name very similar to it."

"I'm going to check the Internet on my mobile phone again, Russ, to see if I can confirm that," Ladybuck adds, as she lifts herself from her seat and strolls down the hallway for some peace and quiet.

Buck calls after her, "Bird! Could you also check where Pyle is buried; that might be important, too!"

Buckminster, "Russell, you know, what your mother said makes me recall having some information about this man. It could be that he was a war correspondent during the last war.

"My granddad told me many years ago that Ernie Pyle was shot on Okinawa by the Japanese toward the end of the fighting in the Pacific theater. I'd forgotten all about that," he concluded.

Ladybird calls from down the hall, "Russell! I have a military Web site on my cell phone. It says 'Ernie Pyle ... war correspondent ... Pulitzer Prize ... World War II ... Japanese shooter ... April 18, 1945 ... Okinawa campaign ... island called Ie Shima ... neighbor island to Okinawa.'

"Buck," she reports, "it says Pyle is buried at the Punchbowl Cemetery in Honolulu."

"Thanks, Bird," Buck acknowledges her research.

"Lynz, try this for DJ," Russell asks. "Can you push the DELTA and 'Page minus' buttons? Just one quick press and let's see what happens,"

"Russell, before Lyndsey does that, you're going to want her to come back to Okinawa later," Ladybuck calls.

In returning from the hallway, she has noted the drift of the conversation.

"We've got to make provision for that.

"She'll have to move one time-click up. Remember, we 'drove' here.

"We all have to make a point of doing that every time we arrive somewhere.

"Each stop we make, unless we arrive with a DELTA click, we need to register that arrival with the *System*, if we think we are going to want to come back to that moment."

James, "Thanks, Dad, and Grandma . . . Alright, Lynz, can you do what Grandma says?

"Hit the DELTA and 'Page minus.' ... Great.

"Now Lyndsey's clicks have brought us back to the middle of the Pacific Ocean.

"Remember, DELTA takes us back to our last time shift, and so we've gone back to the location in the Pacific where Lynz hit the wrong buttons. One of those buttons was obviously a time-shift."

Still viewing the mid-Pacific scene, Russell clarifies, "OK, so the DELTA key isn't going to help us with what is recorded on Pyle's memorial, and we have no way to verify what it says.

"His marker says he died on April 18, 1945, and those guys were behaving as if they had just buried him!

"Back to Okinawa again, Lyndsey, if you would, please," Russell requests.

"Thanks. ... So, Deej, this is Ernie Pyle's memorial on Ie Shima, on or sometime after, April 18, 1945. What we need to know is, how long after?"

"Well," Russell continues, "what is the date here on Shima?

"Thinking about it, I guess the best procedure we have, in order to have accurate time and date info for a visit somewhere, would be to use the journal's calendar or clock, reverse to the date and time we need, and then do the traveling.

"In other words, the *Sunshine-Herald* can only show us the status at the time of our previous visit.

"If we make a time shift while we are away from the journal's offices, we lose the opportunity to get directly back to the paper with the DELTA key.

"Does anyone have a suggestion as to how we can overcome that?"

The gray-headed Richardson is the one who next elects to take the bull by the horns.

Buck picks his way through the legs and feet over to the TV, and, begins a repetition of DJ's extra-vehicular activity of the previous day.

Mirroring the activity of his grandson from his extra vehicular activity, Buckminster first sticks his hand deeply into the screen, withdraws it.

Next, he put his left foot into the HDTV and eases his middle-aged body out of the family room, onto the battle-ravaged island where war correspondent Pyle had taken his last breath.

He quickly, yet carefully, looks around to make sure there are no eyes, and, especially no gun barrels facing his way, then Buck sticks his head back into the room and asks for James' camera, which his wife passes to him.

He strides over to the small wooden marker dedicated to the 44-year-old Dana, Indiana-born man, checks the viewing screen, lines up the camera, and takes a photograph of the humble memorial.

He finishes, as has become the custom by now, by panning around the scene, taking a few seconds of video.

Buck walks to the remnants of the trees and bushes, shot to pieces during the recent brutal fighting, fishes around on the ground.

Moments later he re-emerges holding in his left hand the leather briefcase the 1945-issue American Army officer had thrown there.

His right hand contains none other than an M1911A1 .45-caliber Colt automatic pistol.

Buckminster steps from the violent world of Okinawa of seventy years ago, back into the family room, and is immediately met by James, who takes the .45 pistol out of his grandpa's hand.

James, pistol in hand, steps out of the house, onto the 1945 island through the HD set.

Following his grandfather's example, he takes a rapid, yet cautious glance around to check for possible unwelcome hardware in the area.

Deej proceeds to perform an administrative unload of the pistol.

After pointing the weapon in a safe direction, away from the *System*, and his family, he deftly removes the magazine to get the unfired ammunition out of the handle of the weapon. He slides the clip into his pocket.

"Hey, whaddya think you're doing?" a stentorian voice demands.

A voice belonging to a huge American army sergeant, who now strides into view from behind the portal; a direction in which neither Buck nor Deej had checked.

A teenager holding a .45-caliber automatic pistol under war conditions would normally represent a potential enemy – big time.

Nevertheless, the sergeant has no fear; he knows something of which DJ is completely unaware, but that the lad is about to find out.

The blue jeans and tee shirt the lad is wearing make up an unusual uniform, however, and the big soldier is very curious as to 'what's up' with David James Richardson.

"Why are you out of uniform?" No mention of the pistol the lad is unloading! Is it possible he could have mistaken DJ for an errant soldier playing with an automatic?

"Sorry, Staff, I just arrived on the island and can't find my uniform. I'm a bit disoriented, and I'm starved; could you direct me to where I could get some chow?"

"Sure, young 'un. The mess hall is in that tent over there," he drawls, as he points to a long canvas structure, again to the rear of the *System*.

"They're serving non-stop meals all day today, because the island has just been declared 'safe' by the commanding general. So you can haul yourself over there at your leisure for a meal."

"Swell, Sarge.

"As I mentioned before, I am quite disoriented ... I can't even remember the date ... Can you help me with that?"

Pointing to the Pyle plaque, he says, "See that memorial, son. That happened yesterday, April 18. We just buried the man this morning, April 19."

"Thanks so much, Sarge; I appreciate your help."

The large body disappears out of sight behind the portal, so James continues to unload the automatic pistol.

With his finger positioned alongside the trigger guard, he operates the slide to remove the contents of the firing chamber, which renders the gun completely inert.

Finally, he lowers the hammer gently to its rest position, and picks up the single ejected round of ammunition from the ground.

Our young, international traveler, and first-class diplomat, now returns to the modern-day world. He hands the firearm, and the ejected clip, along with the single .45-caliber round, to his grandfather.

Buck is delighted at recovering his belated souvenirs of the Okinawa campaign; also to have gotten such magnificent items of military hardware at such an incredibly low cost.

"Thanks for doing that, James. I ought to have thought of it myself ... Actually, I should have known better.

"I've wanted to begin a collection of handguns for a long time ... this will make a fine start. I can display these things along with the M-1 Garand clip and the eight cartridge casings young Bartlett James left behind."

The family gathers around to inspect the brand-new artifact and the cartridges retrieved from its inner parts.

"You know, Dad," Lyndsey interjects, "I was about to suggest that the only real way open to us, is to back-pedal to the day or time that Mr. Pyle was actually killed.

"From there we could have moved forward to the point when the group of men around the memorial finally breaks up.

"Then, we would have been able to calculate the exact date of that event. Now, of course, we don't need to do that any more."

"Come on up for lunch, everyone!" Dianne calls down the stairs to the rec room.

"Coming right away!" calls back the straw boss.

James seems to be getting a little more comfortable with his new responsibilities.

First backing off from the Okinawa scene, the group heads off upstairs for a lunch of croissants, ham, cheese, imported pickles, pound cake, angel cake, coffee, tea and other goodies that really hits the spot.

While enjoying the munchies, Lyndsey is running her eyes over the antique leather pouch Buck recovered from the bushes on Ie Shima.

The badly tarnished clasp releases at a touch, and the folder opens to reveal a bundle of both handwritten and typed notes.

There is mention of GIs, grunts, leathernecks and many other references, most of which carry no meaning for Lynz.

"Dad," she asks. "What are the possibilities that these papers are valuable?"

"I'd forgotten about the pouch. I guess it belongs to your granddad; he's the one who found it. Let me look at what you've got there in your hand."

She hands him the pouch, with the papers on top. "Thanks," he acknowledges.

He riffles through the papers, paying particular attention to the signature at the bottom of most pages. "The majority of these is signed

'Ernie Pyle,' with a nice clear signature and a flourish under each name. If these are genuine, they would be a real find."

"What would the Ernie Pyle Museum think about a donation of these papers? That way, the burden of proof would be upon the folks there. Then we would really know whether or not they were genuine," Buckminster volunteers.

"That's a really good suggestion, Gramps," Lyndsey commends.

With everyone partaking of lunch, Ladybuck tries not to appear rude as she continues to look with interest at the digital photograph on the small screen of DJ's camera. Using it, Buckminster had taken the photo of Ernie Pyle's memorial.

It suddenly hits her! "Click!" she beams. "I've got it!" says the Richardson matriarch with glee.

The lunchtime crowd stops its chatter, and gives her its full attention; each one wondering what she has to say.

"It's the uniforms; you noticed that they weren't the same. Young Bartlett James, who almost shot our darling DJ, was with the U.S. Marine Corps.

"The others, the men we just saw, were from the 77th Infantry Division of the U.S. Army. It was the *army* people who erected the Pyle memorial that Buckminster photographed.

"The two groups are from different sections of the American military. They would not necessarily have identical uniforms and battle dress outfits."

"Great spotting, Grandma," Lynz and DJ commend.

Ladybird volunteers, "The military Web site I checked, said that shortly after the Ie Shima fighting was done, the American forces placed a permanent marker there in place of the temporary one.

"That was back in 1945, so if we were to come back there at any time after mid-'45, that new memorial would be in place.

"It apparently still bears exactly the same wording as the wooden one, but it's now a much larger stone marker with a metal plaque attached to it."

Russell queries, "So what you're saying, Mom, is that what we've been looking at is 1945 *before* the stone memorial was positioned there?"

"That's what that Web site seems to indicate. It may be that the monument is still there to this day."

"We need to move ahead a month or so in time; but we can't use our DELTA key to check out the date.

"Anyone have a suggestion as to how we can time-shift ahead to a specific date, without counting the periods of daylight or darkness?" Russell questions.

"You know, what we need is an old watch; one with a calendar display on it." Dianne responds. "Preferably, with 'year' digits included; and still working, otherwise my idea won't work."

"What are you talking about, Dianne," Ladybuck asks.

"There's an old watch like that in my room," DJ volunteers. "I'll go get it." The youngster heads for the stairs.

Dianne, "What I am thinking is, if we can set DJ's obsolete timepiece to a date we know is accurate, and then put it on the ground on Ie Shima, inside the *System*.

"That will put it within the influence of the time shift in the historic scene, and will register according to the passage of time on Ie Shima."

"So, Mom," Russell clarifies for his mother, "We can set the date, even the time, to match what we know of the historic moment on the island, say, for example, April 19.

"From there, we can just run the *System* forward until the date on the old chronometer matches what we're looking for.

"We might go looking for a date in August, or September, for example, of the same year.

"We'll have to run an experiment or two to find out if we can use it to go back to 1945. The movement may not be programmed to show years.

"Even if it does, if it was made in the 1990s, it may only show years starting during that decade, but we can worry about that later.

"Fortunately, in this case, we'll only be moving forward a few months, not years."

James hears some of this explanation as he works his way up to his bedroom to retrieve the aged chronometer.

Returning, he resets its calendar to April 19, the date the big soldier had supplied.

His dad also said the actual year is immaterial, since the time shift is to be only a few weeks.

He hands the watch to his dad, who checks it, then leans into the *System* and gently places it onto the ground on the Okinawan island, with its face still visible to a person looking at it from the house.

Again, U.S. military authorities declared the island safe from April 19 forward, so there shouldn't be any hostile action to threaten the family anyway.

"Lyndsey," Russell asks, "could you please move ahead in time until I tell you to stop. I'm keeping an eye on the old timepiece and I'll let you know when we have moved far enough."

Centering the Pyle memorial marker through the TV screen, our 'chauffeur' complies with his request.

Lyndsey slowly moves forward from April 19, 1945. But, her dad did not need to say stop. The change to the memorial is almost instant.

The Web site report again proves true; just days after the island was declared safe, the plain wooden notice was indeed replaced by a heavy headstone.

Awesome! "Just like you said, Bird," proclaims Buckminster.

"The Pyle marker has changed over from the planks of wood, to a large stone monument with a metal plaque. The same wording is on it," the older man states.

"Better still," James observes. "Don't forget Mom has given us an accurate way for us to time shift for short periods, using the old watch trick. We'll have to keep that in mind."

"Can I offer a suggestion here?" Dianne asks. "I know I recommended it, but, instead of setting the thing on the ground, why don't you bend a coat hanger and place it outside?

"That way, you can hang the timepiece on it facing the 'driver,' and we won't need to stoop over to keep an eye on it."

Suggestion accepted and acted upon immediately.

####

4 "The Collision" in Nowra, Australia

Sunday afternoon, evening, and the better part of Monday morning, have been spent on test runs, tryouts, and practice for those who have not been able to amass much earlier experience.

Both Buckminster and Ladybuck have been sharing in this activity and have quickly acquired the skills necessary to keep the family out of trouble.

No one has bothered with work, housework, or school. All mundane activities have taken a back seat to the *System*.

Voice-mail is up and running, and virtually all telephone calls are being ignored. Something much more fascinating is taking everyone's attention.

Their initial activity involves the date and time.

The group must first get both the newspaper's calendar and clock to match the house data.

James' chronometer remains on the rack on the other side of the portal's screen so that its display will automatically adjust to agree with the other media, including the year.

"Let's reverse in time now," DJ says, taking the touch-pad.

The boy back-pedals in time slowly as February changes into January, then December.

Then, it moves through the fall months of 2014, and into the summer period; but, the battery in the ancient timepiece is beginning to fade.

By the time the display shows April, its lights have gone out.

"I'll have to put another battery in it; I have a spare in my room. Back in a second." The boy heads up to his bedroom again.

With a new battery in place, and with the watch reset to agree with the journal's installation, James again reverses in time.

Back in time to where the battery died, and the display backpedals from April, 2014. James slows to a crawl as the timepiece registers the days of early March, 2012.

He's interested to see if February 29 will show up, indicating that the watch's electronics are even familiar with the concept of leap years, since, in a leap year, that extra day surfaces.

What a delight to see it *does*, and that the watch can handle such idiosyncrasies.

The watch's electronics are apparently programmed to respond to anything involved in the routine measurement of time.

It now continues to roll backward, but only through April, 2009, then the digital display on the timepiece begins to fade again.

It barely reaches January, 2009, when the display once again disappears altogether.

"What's with these batteries? They don't last any time at all," he concludes.

Lyndsey, "I hate to be the bearer of bad tidings, James, but don't forget watch batteries last for only five years.

"Outside in the *System*, you're going through five years in about five seconds flat. Do you have a way to plug it into the house current?"

"I could hardwire it, DJ," Grandpa Buckminster volunteers. "But, I won't be able to do it without my soldering iron; unless *you* have one, Russell."

"I do have one, Dad. Can I give you a hand with it in the workshop downstairs?"

The two senior Richardsons head off to the workshop, with ancient timepiece in hand.

This will involve precision soldering. Inside the battery compartment of a wristwatch, there is little room for maneuvering.

#

The two elders surface again after an absence of about twenty minutes, bearing the watch, which now has a hole drilled in its back through which two wires protrude, one red, one black.

"How did you manage to do that, Dad," Dianne asks.

"Wasn't too hard," Buck replies. "Russell pried the terminals from horizontal into an upright position and insulated them from touching each other.

"All I had to do was use his soldering iron to attach a wire to each one. It was simple to drill a hole in the back to pass the two wires through.

"All we need now is a step down transformer that works on house current and that puts out 1.55 volts DC," the older Richardson concludes.

"Gramps, I have something that might help," Lyndsey offers.

"In my room, I have a travel converter I bought last year; it's good for American and European input, either 110 or 220 volts, and has an adjustable output that, I think, goes down to 1.5 volts. Would that help?"

"That might be good enough," which sets Lynz running for the upper reaches of the house. Moments later, she reappears bearing a small box with the electrical device inside.

Back off to the workshop go the seniors bearing their latest toy. They surface after a further ten minutes with large smiles on their faces.

"Can we start this trial run over again?" Russell asks.

With the *Sunshine-Herald*'s display still on the screen, the newspaper's clock and calendar are once adjusted back to match the information on show on the wall of the rec room.

The watch, powered up once again, is first adjusted by hand to match the other two sources.

Now, with the timepiece in plain sight, in situ on the 'James rack,' they once again proceed to work backward from 2015.

The batteries have been eliminated and this time the watch is on house power.

James' watch was manufactured some twenty-five years ago, in 1991, and the fear is that it will not display years earlier than 1991. So, this is the item of principal interest.

Inexorably backward, the newspaper's display flashes through the days, weeks and months of each year.

2014, 2013, 2012 ... 2009, 2008, 2007 ... 1994, 1993, 1992. Our corporate wristwatch matches the journal's clock beat for beat.

The boy slows as he sees the chronometer working its way down to January, 1991 ... March, February, January.

Then, December, 1990, at which point, the newspaper's display changes from digital over to analog. The big elongated hands are back.

He now can feel comfortable speeding up once the watch rolls over the anticipated stop date. The huge arms of the journal's clock are a blur as they swirl the years away.

What fascinates also is the way the newspaper offices shrink in size, as the years peel away the upgrades the corporation had made to its edifice in earlier times.

It continues, passing 1989, 1988, 1987. When the aged watch and newspaper displays both show January 1, 1950, he finally stops.

He calls out for his grandmother the numbers '1-9-4-1' and 'ENTER,' as he punches that same sequence on the touch-pad.

The response is instantaneous as the time on both sources indicates January 1, 1941.

"'1-8-8-1' and ENTER." Again, an immediate response, from both the timepiece and the journal's calendar. Both rip over to exactly the date requested. The default for this action is January 1.

"Anyone any idea why this is working, when this watch has no idea that the year 1881 existed in U.S. history?" the puzzled lad asks.

"The LCD display of the watch must contain all the elements to create the digits, as well as the electronic circuitry to drive it; you are simply using them all.

"The device just shows you what date it is, without any questions or arguments." Grandma Ladybuck is on the ball once again.

"OK, if that's the way it is, then we have found the way to get around in time, without ever having to resort to unnecessarily counting light and dark periods. Thanks to you, Mom."

#

DJ is thinking that it is about time to do some traveling, maybe even big time!

"Dad, do you think we could use the *System* to go to some air shows in the summer?"

"For sure," Russell responds. "We can do anything you want, as long as it's still working.

"The real beauty of the *System* is that, if we want to, we can back-pedal to World War II, and actually watch those aircraft literally performing the deeds for which they are now revered.

"For instance, there is nothing at all to prevent us from taking a trip back to the South Pacific and following the planes on the 'Doolittle Raid.'

"We could even fly with the squadrons of aircraft as they took part in the 'Great Marianas Turkey Shoot.'

"We can fly as 'chase plane' with the Lancaster bombers on the 'Dam Busters' raid as it unfolded over Germany."

"There are other things we could check out too," Ladybuck adds. "Actually, I have a few suggestions that I could make for projects.

"I know the Washington Monument is made from stone of two or three different shades of color, and I know *why* from my history classes.

"However, it would be a real hoot to be there in the eighteen-seventies and eighties.

"We could oversee them actually building the obelisk; and find out what the architects and engineers thought of the 'new' load of stone when they installed it and noticed the color difference.

"Too," she appends, "the 'White House,' also in Washington, was originally made of sandstone, which can be anywhere from white to red in color.

"So why is the building painted white today? The answer to that question is about two hundred years old. It would be interesting to be able to visit the men who did that, and see what happened to create that change."

"Grandma," James says, "that's a great idea about the Washington Monument. I like that.

"Those are all places we will definitely go and check on in the days ahead. Keep coming up with the suggestions. I came up with a few things we could check out, too." the teen adds.

"But we do need to do more testing first. We could be wasting a lot of time doing things the wrong way round, or perhaps because we don't recognize shortcuts; as was the case with the DELTA button for example."

"Actually, Dad, it wasn't really an air show I wanted to go to. I had a specific place in mind that I would like visit, and something we could have a look at, Dad."

"Alright, what did you have in mind, son?"

"How would you like to check out a 'PBY' in mint condition? It'll give us an opportunity to do a long-range sortie.

"It would be our first intentional trip overseas where we genuinely go somewhere out of choice, not necessity. We might even be able to check out some of the scenery along the way."

"Sounds great, but … international?" Russell questions. "Long range? … Where on earth is it? … What's your idea of long range?"

"The place I wanted to go to is called Nowra? We can have a close-up look at the Catalina that's on display in the airplane museum there?"

"Where?"

"Nowra … New South Wales … It overlooks Jervis Bay on the east coast of Australia, about 100 miles south of Sydney."

Russell, "OK, Deej, you're the boss; but, how did you find out about this aircraft, if it's in Australia?"

"I stumbled over it on a Web site on my mobile the other day."

"Do you mind if I drive, Dianne?"

"Not at all, Russ. I should be doing some prep work on our lunch now, anyway. Could you call me right away if anything interesting comes up?" With that, handing the remote touch-pad over to her husband, she takes her leave upstairs to the kitchen.

First, we turn our attention back to the newspaper, to DELTA-key our way back from the 1880s, to insure the date and time match the information on display in the family room.

Once the huge analog clock disappears, and the huge digital display device returns to their view, both it and the corporate watch are finally adjusted to show Monday, February 23, 2015, 11:45 a.m.

Because of the difference in time between southeastern Australia and St. Pete's, Russell elects to arrive in Australia in daylight.

Thus, he 'shifts' the *System* into reverse, and backs up quickly until the journal's information shows February 22, 11:45 p.m., a loss of twelve hours.

Daylight almost instantly vanishes, rapidly turning to blackness as the sun, in fast-rewind mode, quickly falls into the eastern sky, dragging with it the light of dawn until it changes into intense darkness.

The view is a darkened Tampa Bay, with city lights shimmering on the water as the family heads out. Nightlife lovers' automobiles light the surfaces of the area's multiple causeways.

Their track is north northeast, on a trip of roughly 185 miles to Jacksonville.

Once there, the kids' dad turns the portal to travel due west for about 330 miles from Jacksonville to Pensacola, in the Florida Panhandle.

Like an expert, Russell continues across the north coast of the Gulf of Mexico, passing over Houston, Texas, then west-northwest for the final portion of the U.S. sector of their trip.

It is well over 1,000 miles from Houston to San Diego, and, after almost clipping the U.S./Mexican border at El Paso, Texas, the California coastline of the United States passes below.

A slight turn to port and the family is on its way across the Pacific Ocean once again; this time in the direction of Australia's southeast coastline, vectoring a smidgen south of Honolulu, HI.

Outside 14 Dusty Miller Drive, their home, it is total darkness at just minutes before midnight when they left.

Now, they are in search of daylight as they chase the westward movement of the sun's rays.

Past Hawaii, where it is just time for sunset, they perform a fly-by of the International Date Line, before slipping over Nadi, Fiji (or, Nandi, as the Fijians call it).

Russell adjusts to a southwestern trajectory and the really big island comes into sight.

Since the east coast of Australia is visible, an important course correction can be made. Russ makes a turn above the Coral Sea toward Australia's principal metropolis.

Aiming roughly south, over Queensland's Gold Coast, and the Great Barrier Reef, the folks first pass by the city of Brisbane.

Now the family is well on its way to the Nowra area.

As the *System* surges toward the south, the six eager tourists arrive over the state of New South Wales, and Sydney comes into view.

Russell slows down, allowing everyone to enjoy the gorgeous sights.

Sydney's famous Opera House is to be seen gleaming in the brilliant sunshine of a beautiful Oz afternoon.

Its neighbor, the Sydney Harbour Bridge, stands majestically on the fascinating waterfront.

For almost ninety years, it has been standing guard as fleets of ferries endlessly made their way in and out of the harbour, traveling from and to their points of departure and destination.

Then, they continue on a southern vector over the spectacularly Edenic view from Bulli Lookout, at the northern end of Wollongong, and past the massive steelworks at Port Kembla.

Still heading southward, the male Generation X-er makes a slight turn inland to get a look at Albion Park Rail's small but burgeoning civil airfield.

Initially glimpsing it in the near distance, with its adjacent bedroom community of the same name, he thinks it might be worth a visit.

He notes to his dad and DJ the aircraft-restoration facility at the edge of the field.

As the *System* passes silently overhead, the 'inmates' at the nursing home sit comfortably in their seats, and wheelchairs, in the residents' lounge at No. 2 Pine Street, where lunch is just a memory, while dinner is a colorful dream.

The group passes down an imaginary line between Theodore Street and Central Avenue in Oak Flats. Wentworth, Parkes, and Lyne Streets zip silently beneath.

Then, once over Lake Illawarra, a turn to starboard returns them to the ocean, another allows them to resume their southbound course out over the Pacific once more.

Their vector gives them the opportunity to make an overflight of Shellharbour's near-empty beaches; over the 'world-famous blowhole' at Kiama.

Finally, the sweeping curve of Jervis Bay causes the group to again catch its collective breath at the area's awe-inspiring beauty.

After their under-three-minute trip from Tampa Bay, they arrive at their ultimate destination.

Though it is February, mid-summer in Australia, with the sun still high in the sky, it is nonetheless relatively quiet on the beaches.

With the fourteen-hour time difference from the darkness of St. Pete's, on a Monday afternoon in Nowra, at 1:50 p.m., folks are back at their workplaces. Hence, lunchtime is about over in the Shoalhaven region of Australia's sunshine coast.

As this is a weekday, there yet remains about an hour before the kids start showing up at the beach from school, at around 15:00, as is their custom.

Naturally, they are going to be ready for the necessary, with 'schoolbooks under one arm and surfboard under the other.'

"DJ, perhaps you had better take over from here. I'm not the best at the detailed stuff." Russell hands off the touch-pad to DJ.

At a low rate of knots, James 'banks' over the Pacific Ocean (in this area, it is called the Tasman Sea,) and heads inland, due west, just twelve miles to a military airfield, HMAS *Albatross*.

Touchdown! This marks their arrival at the museum home of a said-to-be spectacular copy of the Consolidated PBY.

Visitors scurry around both the interior and exterior display areas, inspecting the various artifacts belonging to the flight museum.

"Dad, we have to do something about all these visitors."

"I agree. What about backing up to last night; then we can look around at our leisure?"

"Hold on, Russell," says Ladybird Richardson. "You've been jiggling around with the clock already. I've kept track of each change that's been made so far, and I might be able to save you from getting confused.

"When you're ready … we started out on Monday, February 23, at 11:45 a.m. From that, you deducted twelve hours in order to arrive in Oz in daylight.

"That put us to Sunday, February 22 at 11:45 p.m. in St Pete's.

"If we add fourteen hours to that to extrapolate it over from our time, to Australian eastern daylight time, it gives us 1:45 p.m. in Nowra, on Monday afternoon, the twenty-third.

"A DELTA over to the newspaper now, will verify that exactly, but the clock on the wall shows that my notes are only a minute or two out and that's going to be the amount of time we spent traveling.

"So, if DJ can move back in time for thirty-six hours, (which will leave us a total of forty-eight hours off the actual time,) that will put us back on the week-end at close to 2:00 a.m.

"Sunday morning at Nowra, and, voila, no museum visitors."

"Bird, that's brilliant." Buckminster commends his wife.

David James Richardson clicks just once on the DELTA and 'Page minus' keys to expose the *Sunshine-Herald*'s offices.

Because all the time-slot changes had been made prior to departing St. Pete's, after extrapolating the data over to NSW time, the journal's digital timepiece identifies the local time in St. Pete's, their base time, as being almost exactly what Ladybuck had predicted.

James' wrist chronometer verifies the information is accurate to the minute.

A press on the DELTA and 'Page plus,' and the family's view changes back to the Naval Air Station at Nowra once more.

"Dad," DJ asks, as he moves the *System* to an obscure location, to be out-of-sight to possible onlookers, and lowers the portal down to ground level, "could you double-check me with the watch.

"Keep your eye on it with me outside on the rack, so that we can make sure I go thirty-six hours, and not any further?"

Russell knows the obsolete timepiece is going to be their only reliable reference for their Nowra visit, and that it will need to be adjusted to match Oz time.

The senior Richardson first clears this with his son, who agrees to the change.

Russ makes the correction so that the watch shows local time, just for the sake of doing things in an orderly manner.

Hence, it now displays 1:56 p.m. on Monday, February 23, 2015.

James reverses rapidly for a day and a half, while his old timepiece moves through a full thirty-six hours, and eventually shows the time to be around 1:56 a.m., and its calendar indicates Sunday, February 22, 2015.

Russell is able to verify that his son has not gone beyond the 36-hour mark.

It is fascinating to think that in the final second of their time shift, the sun zipped back beneath the western horizon, and the sky flashed from brilliant sunshine through pre-dawn light of morning and then to total darkness.

At the Nowra facility, the Southern Cross is clearly to be seen in the night sky of what DJ now knows for sure is within mere minutes of 2:00 a.m., Sunday morning.

The 36-hour time reversal strategy is a great success; the museum's visitors simply disappear.

Atypically (as their luck has held out incredibly well to date), the big Cat they have come so far to see is nowhere in sight.

The refurbished aircraft must be in one of what seem to be the museum's hangars, near the main gates of the naval air station.

So, in Nowra's deep darkness, James 'helicopters' slowly around the base, checking for some indication as to where the Cat might be.

"Perhaps there is a sign," someone volunteers.

James hovers back to the main gates, peering into the new nighttime darkness; again, the security men are completely unaware of the presence of this new 'stealth' device.

James is still scanning for signs that indicate where the Catalina aircraft might be hiding.

"<u>JAMES! LOOK OUT FOR THAT HANGAR!</u>"

Too late! At full tilt, the group ploughs into a museum hangar ... What now? ... What is damaged?

Even more crucial, how will its operational capabilities be affected? ... Can it still be used to 'drive' home? ... How will it respond to efforts to move about in future time-travel missions?

The portal, from the view of its passengers inside the house, appears unharmed, but initially the unit will need to be lowered to the ground to permit an inspection of the exterior.

Incredibly, on the house side, the *System* appears intact, despite a strike of such magnitude.

Especially is the group grateful for the fact that no one has been hurt in the silent 'collision.'

As paradoxical as it may seem, the portal has passed completely through the solid wall of the airplane hangar, apparently without damage to the building, or, more importantly to the family, or to the *System*.

"Dad, look at that old Sea Venom! What beautiful condition!"

"Never mind that, James! How on earth did we get through that wall without getting the portal damaged or destroyed?"

James rotates until the point of impact with the hangar comes into view. Finding: The building is totally unscathed!

"You'd better call your mother down here, Lyndsey. She'll need to be in on this. We may have wrecked the *System*!"

"Can you drop us down onto the ground, Deej?"

"We're already on the deck, Dad," the boy confirms. Since no one from the Naval Air Station is within sight or earshot, Russell climbs off the still-shattered sofa.

The adult ducks down and clambers, right foot first, through the plasma TV, onto the sealed concrete floor of the airplane museum at HMAS *Albatross*.

Dianne arrives on the lower level in time to see the back end of her husband disappearing into the ether.

"Be careful out there, Russ," she cautions.

"What's happened?" she inquires of the remaining members of the group. "Why is Russell going out?"

"James ran into a hangar wall, but we seem to have passed right through it without any damage to the *System*. Dad's gone out to inspect it for us."

Lyndsey is succinct in her reply; nonetheless, Dianne appears content with the response.

The first thing is to take a look around the exterior of the portal, to make sure that damage, if any, is minimal.

Russell has long legs, which could carry him in very short order around the time machine.

However, he chooses to circle the device twice, slowly, just to be sure. It truly seems wondrous, like a miracle has happened, inasmuch as damage is zero; totally absent.

Now Dad will make a move toward the real purpose of the trip. Russell sticks his head back into the room, and says to James, "Let me just do this, and I'll be back."

His head exits the house, and then, at a range of exactly 9,287 miles from home, an arm reaches back into the Florida homestead, and picks Lyndsey's camera from atop the large-screen TV.

Russ strides closer to the De Havilland DH-112 Sea Venom, Mark FAW-53, and from various angles takes several photographs of the long-immobile airplane.

He chooses not to use the flash in order to avoid alerting the station's security guards.

Now, while walking slowly around the formerly carrier-borne artifact, he takes one minute or so of low-lux video, stopping briefly every few seconds as he strolls around the beautifully restored and maintained museum piece.

Completing that task, within thirty seconds he is physically back inside the house in St. Pete's.

However, the near-disaster is a serious event that needs some discussion. "Maybe it would be good to bring the *System* back home, James. You'll need to re-think this operation very carefully.

"We can always come back here later, if we decide to pursue seeing the Cat.

"Perhaps next time one of us should go for a spacewalk on Shank's pony and find the plane first, so that we can check it out at our leisure."

DJ makes the trip back to St. Pete's by the use of the DELTA key. The first DELTA, accompanied by a 'Page minus,' takes the group back to the beginning of the thirty-six hour time shift.

The second returns the family to its 'default' location, facing the journal's edifice back at home.

Therefore, comparing notes when they arrive at their local newspaper they find that, no matter what any of the clocks might indicate, less than forty-five minutes has elapsed since the group initially left home on its trip to Nowra.

There is also the matter of the twelve hours Russell back-pedaled at the outset, to permit arrival in Oz during daylight.

For the time being the journal clock is ignored, and the folks are guided by the rec room clock.

Indeed, the DELTA is proving true the prediction of James, who identified it as a function that would, in future operations, prove to be very valuable.

#

Next time they go on any trip, they'll be trying to complete it without incident. Everyone will readily agree with this determination.

"DJ, that DELTA button is proving to be really handy," Dianne comments. "If you want to, you can leave the *System* on that display and just zip back to Nowra later.

"That will save you having to make any time consuming changes.

"Anyway, the wall clock says that it's time for lunch. Any complaints?"

"Awesome!" The vote is unanimous.

"Deej, are you OK with talking about that collision at *Albatross*, after we eat?"

"Maybe during lunch, Dad; since we'll have everyone present at the same time."

#

Between bites, "Dad, after we collided with that hangar wall, you walked around the outside of the portal to do a visual check. What did you find?"

"Great question, Deej; good for you," Buck pipes in.

Russell, "Well, that was the strange thing about it. The inside wall of the hangar was completely unmarked and there wasn't a single scratch on the exterior of the *System*."

"So, does that mean the *System* has the ability to pass through solid objects without any ill effects?" Lyndsey asks.

Ladybird, "Why don't you ease it across the street, and see if you make a lasting impression on the clock display at the newspaper?"

"What a fine suggestion, and we wouldn't have to 'drive' far to try that out."

#

"Thanks for lunch, Mom; that was great!" One pleasant hour at chow, and much conversation later, we are back at the HDTV ready for the big experiment.

"I know I was 'driving' when we hit the hangar at Nowra, but, maybe it's best I do this one.

"Or, maybe, better still, Lyndsey should take a crack at it. She knows as much about this as I do; so why not?"

"Thanks, Deej; this is challenging," his sister says.

Now in charge of the remote, Lyndsey gently eases the portal across Second Street South, and aims the HDTV directly at the center of the huge calendar display.

It has the appearance of the jumbo fluorescent screens where scores are exhibited for sports fans at a ballpark.

As the family moves in closer and closer, Lynz slows down to allow everyone to be able to observe the full effects of the 'collision.'

The *System* touches the sign and the whole group holds its collective breath as the HDTV slips ever so smoothly into, and then, gently, completely through the sign.

Not a sound is heard as the large-screen device easily penetrates even the glass portions of the metal-backed sign.

Forward motion terminates with a brief view inside the newspaper's offices, from which Lyndsey tactfully extracts the group before the building's staff catches sight of the family.

This fascinating experiment verifies a paradoxical possibility.

It now surfaces that the *System* provides the folks with a means of passing through solid structures.

This development further helps illustrate for the family the need for caution as to putting out word of the existence of the *System*.

Once public knowledge of the phenomenon is a reality, a capability of this nature would automatically make the portal of extreme interest to those with criminal minds.

That is why David James Richardson earlier referred to such ones as the 'bad guys out there.'

#

The lunchtime pow-wow is over, and the sign-penetration question is resolved.

Now Lyndsey thoughtfully recommends an immediate return to Nowra to try again to let the boys see the Catalina.

"Thanks, LP; that's very kind of you to make that suggestion.

"It's only a couple of DELTA and 'Page +' key presses to get there, and we now know how we can time-shift to ease the problems created by our running into crowds of people."

He continues, "I'm all for accepting that idea. As a matter of fact, I would like you to be our 'driver' because you did such a good job on the newspaper's clock display."

Lyndsey uses the two stabs at the DELTA combination of buttons on the remote control to 'zip' the group back to Nowra.

This time, given a choice, despite having to delve around in the post-midnight darkness of 1:50 a.m., she chooses to start the family's search by 'intruding' into the same hangar into which her brother had 'crashed' earlier.

Thanks to the reasonably adequate lighting in the hangar, the teen immediately recognizes the De Havilland Sea Venom that her dad had checked out and photographed on their earlier trip.

She remembers, too, that there is no Catalina here.

James' watch remains positioned on the rack inside the *System*, just past the screen, while he remains inside the house, with the timepiece well within the girl's sight.

The teen, realizing that running around in the dark between the hangars is getting her nowhere, asks DJ for permission to make a time shift. She's thinking a later hour will be better, when no members of the public are around.

With DJ's OK, Lynz 'departs' from the hangar and 'intrudes' on the Security office back at the main gate.

Lyndsey has in mind a very logical maneuver; a forward time shift to a moment when daylight is extant, but prior to the arrival of the day's visitors.

With guard personnel unaware of their presence, the teen gets into a position allowing her to see both the office calendar and clock.

This enables her to 'advance' about four and one-half hours to sunrise. [At this time of year, sunrise in New South Wales is around 6:30 a.m.]

Once the clock indicates that it is after sunrise, yet still before the museum's opening hours, with daylight visible through the windows, she reckons that this will be perfect.

The girl's dad is about to make changes to the newly-hotwired timepiece, just for their common reference, when he remembers that it is on-site in NSW and needs no changes to be made.

Lyndsey now 'extracts' the *System* from Security and … *voila*, … broad daylight … yet no visitors.

So, the teenager 'chauffeurs' the family over to the first hangar where she thinks there could be museum aircraft displayed.

Again, she 'intrudes,' but this time, at the spot where the roof joins the wall. This height, on one of the 'short' walls, seems to be the optimum.

This vantage point offers sufficient elevation to enable the group to be able to see most of the contents of the hangar at a single glance.

Still 'no dice.' The hangar is filled with, not ancient aircraft, but, rather, modern fighter aircraft. No sign of the Cat.

Again, she 'withdraws' from the Naval Air Station's second hangar and moves on to the third and final hangar. Once more, no Catalina; only helicopters.

"This is disappointing," Lyndsey thinks to herself. "Where can the veteran Catalina be hiding?"

Bingo! As she 'extracts' the *System* from the last hangar, she spots a possible location. The hangar, where they had seen the Sea Venom fighter, is much longer on the outside than the exhibition area they had found inside on their earlier visits.

Hence, the hangar with which James had originally 'collided' was the next stop. The teenager draws up at the outer wall of the hangar where their 'impact' had occurred and 'intrudes' as usual.

No Catalina; but that's OK with Lynz.

She now realizes that the museum hangar has two sections, with a huge bulkhead wall between them. The wall has a small personnel door in it, but this is hidden behind an aircraft that is part of the display.

It takes but a moment to pass from the first section through the wall to the second area, and, '*eureka.*' One 'Consolidated Aircraft' PBY-6A, vintage 1945.

"Can you drop us down to the floor, Lyndsey?" Russell asks.

As she complies with Dad's request, each of the guys heads for the HDTV with the intent of taking a hike over to the PBY.

Both digital cameras quickly go into action as the men-folk disembark from the portal, and inspect every feature of the archived aircraft.

There is more than enough ambient natural light to support the photography.

A series of pictures is taken: the floats; the observers' bubbles; the wheel wells; the outside of the cockpit; the wing configuration, and the hull.

Next, from a short distance, both cameras move into the video mode, and then busy themselves recording the full length and wingspan of the World War II artifact.

Finally, the fin, rudder and tail plane are the subject of the cameras; in particular, both dwell briefly upon the aircraft's registration (VH-PBZ) and its other markings (A24-362, OX-V).

Re-embarkation is with reluctance. Although delight glows on their faces, they re-enter the house with their joy tempered by feelings of regret at having to leave the big bird.

"Well, at least we'll have the pictures and the video," they console themselves.

After the lads have spent well over an hour ogling and stroking the old warbird, Ladybuck offers to make coffee and tea for everyone, including those visiting the museum.

All agree whole-heartedly. "I thought you'd never ask!" says one, in jest. The matron heads off upstairs in the direction of the kitchen.

#

"Ready, you guys!" Ladybird Richardson calls down the stairs.

Those in the rec room start up the stairs, and, most of those giving attention to the aircraft return to the house without delay.

Everyone makes for the aroma of coffee in the dining room, with the sole exception of Buck. While everyone else has disappeared, the Richardson patriarch remains behind, still gazing at the museum's static display of planes.

He stares at an S-2 Tracker as if he had never seen one before.

#

The old twin-radial-engined, carrier-borne airplane, which Buckminster knows first entered service with the U.S. Navy in 1954 as its first purpose-built ASW (anti-submarine-warfare) aircraft, had been bought by the Royal Australian Navy starting from 1967.

Buck also remembers hearing the news that, in the mid seventies, an arsonist lit a fire in a particularly bad spot. It destroyed a large number of the Australian complement of Trackers, right where he is standing, *Albatross*.

The loss of the Trackers had been particularly badly felt at the RAN, and orders were sent out to purchase some previously owned U.S. Navy S-2 Trackers to replace them.

He also knew these were subsequently received and put into service with the Australian Navy. They remained on the active inventory until 1984.

#

He suddenly appears to make a decision, and picks up DJ's camera and heads for the HDTV. He ducks down and disembarks from the house back into the Nowra hangar.

Buck strides over to the plane and begins to take pictures of the Tracker, paying especial attention to the hydraulic mechanism exposed at the point where the wings would fold for stowage onboard an aircraft carrier.

#

Because Buck is missing from the coffee break upstairs, Dianne strolls unhurriedly down the stairs, sees nothing and presumes her father-in-law is in the rest room.

She checks the washroom on that level, but 'no joy.' The door is open, and no Buckminster.

She glances over at the *System*; sees only the Nowra museum.

She picks up the remote control and, without thinking, presses the DELTA and 'Page plus' keys several times. She stops when the TV reverts to the *Sunshine-Herald* newspaper in St. Pete's.

She replaces the touch-pad in its previous location, and then looks briefly down the stairs to the carport door but to no avail.

"You there, Dad?" she calls, but no reply.

The coffee and other goodies are proving to be a hit with all in the group.

Dianne heads back off upstairs, verifies her husband's father is not in one of the upstairs restrooms, then returns to the coffee crowd.

She says to her mother-in-law, "Mom, what's happened to Buck. I can't find him.

"I thought he had stayed downstairs for a minute or two, but I just went down and looked but I didn't find him in the rec room. I checked down at the carport door and there's no sign of him."

"Oh, don't worry about him; he's probably gone for a stroll. He'll be back in a few minutes. He sure won't want to miss his coffee."

#

Half an hour later, still no Buckminster. Coffee is over and the group is heading back downstairs.

Russell keeps going all the way down to the carport. The door is still locked, but he disengages the lock anyway, walks outside, and around the house, re-enters the house and re-engages the lock.

He is thoughtful as he walks back upstairs to the rec room. "I've tried all around the house and I don't see any sign of Dad," he reports.

"This is beginning to get serious," is the consensus.

"Well, what could have happened to him?" Dianne is starting to worry about her father-in-law. "He dragged his feet a bit when Ladybuck called us up for coffee.

"Two or three minutes later, I came down here to look for him. I checked all around in here, including the restroom, and I couldn't see any sign of him."

#

Meanwhile, literally half a world away, Buck is still innocently taking photos of the Tracker, blithely unaware of the fact that he has been left behind in Australia by a triple click of the DELTA button combo by his Florida family.

After some twenty pictures of the S-2, Buck glances at his wristwatch out of habit. Realizing that more time has passed than he thought, he walks slowly around the Tracker and makes a video record of the aircraft's features.

He turns back to the *System*, or at least to where it was standing when he disembarked from it earlier.

Nothing!

Buckminster stays cool and doesn't panic. "Someone's probably 'driving' around looking for me," he reasons.

Thinking logically, he heads for an open space in the middle of the hangar, hoping he is exposing his whereabouts to whoever is the 'chauffeur.'

Still nothing. He looks carefully around the museum for the near-invisible portal, but to no avail. The time-travel device is nowhere to be found.

Buck is not yet seriously concerned. He realizes that eventually his family will miss him and come looking for him, and settles in for the wait.

#

In Florida, Ladybird and Dianne are beginning to worry. It has already been over an hour since Buckminster disappeared. This concern is reflected in their eyes.

"Dad, why don't we use the *System* to check what happened to Grandpa Buck?" Deej asks.

Russell takes the remote control for the large-screen TV, and seeing the *Sunshine-Herald* through the screen, he says, "We don't need to worry about the time on the journal clock.

"We should check what's going on in Nowra; just to be sure," he asserts.

He clicks the DELTA and 'Page +' buttons and 'zips' the remaining members of the group back to the Oz museum on the other side of the world.

The final stop is the Security Office where Lyndsey had made a change, allowing them to be in increasing daylight and able to search the museum without the annoyance of visitors.

Next, the search for Buckminster will have to follow the route Lynz had taken in her search for the Catalina earlier.

First, he heads off toward the far end of the museum hangar where the Cat and the S-2 Tracker are located. Like his daughter, he 'penetrates' the building at its far end, which he knows is the last place his dad had been seen.

The graceful Catalina is slightly off-center of the screen, while to the right appears the Tracker exhibit that so intrigued Buckminster.

Russell 'rotates' the *System* slowly so that the family is able to look around the remainder of the exhibits and there, in the middle of the floor, stands none other than his dad.

"Over here, Dad," Russell calls.

Buckminster calmly walks over to the portal, looks inside, and proclaims, "I guess I missed coffee, huh?"

"I'll make you a fresh pot, Buckminster," Ladybird volunteers.

"Sounds good," he proclaims, re-embarking into the family room.

"How did you get back to the museum, Gramps?" Lyndsey asks.

"Well, I just climbed through the screen. I saw something of interest and fancied taking extra pictures.

"So, with you all disappearing upstairs, I thought I'd quickly check out the Tracker aircraft and take a few pictures, and I forgot what time it was."

"Were you scared, Gramps?" she ventures.

"Not really. I knew you'd be back for me," Buck assures.

"Oh no!" comes from Dianne. "That was my fault. When I came back downstairs to look for you, Buck, I picked up the remote control and dinged the DELTA button a couple of times. The *System* just reverted over to the journal's display.

"It never dawned on me for one second that someone had gone out of the house back to the museum. I'm so sorry, Dad," she concludes.

Ladybuck appears to be taking this in stride, and seems little concerned about the catastrophe that might have overtaken her husband of forty years.

"Imagine what would have happened if we had not thought to check the museum before looking elsewhere," she calls down the stairs. "You would have been the first man in history to be 'lost in time,'" she jests.

"Hey, we were all looking for you here, so officially, you probably would qualify for that title," James adds.

"Can I add that to my masters degree, after my name?" Buck jokes.

"Coffee's ready, Buckminster!" Ladybuck calls down.

Buck is now the guest of honor on the upper level as his wife serves him with the coffee and goodies he missed earlier.

#

When the telephone rings, someone picks up the cordless device and sees the name Grover; Dianne's folks, so, for a change, it gets answered.

"Hello. Oh, how are you, Dad! No, we're all fine, thanks. We've just been a bit busy for the last little while. Sorry we didn't call you and Mother."

"No, we've been having … uh … a little challenge with our new TV. I think we should have it all fixed up shortly, though. Why, what's happened? … How are the Brownings managing?"

"That's lousy luck, getting a power cut just when they would need to use their air conditioning! … What was that click, Dad? … Is that your call-waiting signal? … OK, if you have to go, say Hi to Mother for all of us, and we'll talk to you very soon. Bye for now."

"Russell, my dad just called to say that the news networks are reporting a tropical storm has made landfall in South Carolina.

"Apparently, it's caused a major power cut to most of the state. It seems the Brownings are OK, so my family members haven't been harmed at all.

"It's just that they've lost their electrical power and aren't able to run their A/C and, as usual, it's quite warm in 'golfers' heaven' right now."

"Gosh, Di, that never even dawned on me! That could cripple us! A power shortage; a brownout; an outright power cut.

"That could be instantly catastrophic for the *System*! … Any one of them! … If that happened to us … Holy smokes! … We'd probably lose the whole thing!"

"Hey! Never mind losing the *System*!" James hollers, "You might lose me! What would happen if I was outside somewhere in the past? How would I get back home again if the power suddenly went off?"

"So," Russell continues, "we're going to have to make some purchases urgently, A gas-driven generator, for starters.

"Plus we'd better get an uninterruptible power source, one of those like the one I have in the office, which is hooked up to my computer, to stop the hard-drive from crashing when the power grid goes down."

"Dad, something else you should maybe think about buying; we badly need a small TV, so that we can watch it here in the rec room. The big TV is kinda spoken for right now," DJ adds.

"We ought to be keeping an eye out for stories like this ourselves, while we're spending our time working with the big screen.

"We can watch National News Network, or some other news outlet. That way, at least we'll be able to latch onto these alerts, without being reliant on Granddad Grover to call."

"OK, that sounds like a pretty good suggestion, Deej. I'll do that."

#

"We'll be back as soon as we can. Call us on my mobile if you think of anything else. Be careful with that thing and don't go through the screen for anything while your mom and I are out."

#

"CURSE THAT GUY! Some jerk just drove off in our SUV.

"He's stolen it out of our carport. I didn't hear the alarm go off … he probably knew how to silence it … a professional.

"LYNDSEY! Can you call '9-1-1' for me?"

"Dad, Lynz and I have the *System* up and running here. Which way did the guy go? We can go after him."

"East on Dusty Miller Drive, and it looks as if he's turning left toward First Avenue North, and he's probably heading for the I-275," Russell calls up the stairs.

"OK, Dad, we're on it! Lyndsey is already cruising down Dusty Miller and rounding the corner to get on First Avenue North. This shouldn't take long."

The *System* performs flawlessly, as it has on every other occasion they have called on it.

Russell and Dianne are coming back upstairs to the rec room to catch the action.

The felonious sinner is already in sight driving the vehicle that he has just 'borrowed' from the Richardson's carport.

He is moving very quickly using the pattern of one-way streets set up by the City of St. Petersburg to help the flow of traffic in the direction of the major freeways.

If he gets to the Interstate-375, he'll be able to access the I-275.

Then, it's only a matter of time until he accesses the Interstate-75 and probably be lost forever, to have his wicked way with Russell's Jeep..

However, that evildoer has no clue that he is under surveillance by six leading-edge 'G-men' from the Richardson's hyper-private detective agency.

As they continue with the operation, they are certainly giving new meaning to the expression 'working undercover.'

Lyndsey is getting to be very skilled at operating the remote; in fact, she has improved drastically since the early 'driving' lessons off Iwo Jima.

The vehicle and its unseen escort now smoothly transition from Fifth Avenue North onto the westbound I-375. With little but open road ahead of him, Mr. Felonious now guns the engine to reach the full Interstate speed limit.

Lynz keeps pace without missing a beat. She carefully 'nudges' the control to continue on a straight path; initially following close behind the Jeep..

The teenager then quickly allows the *System* to pass beyond the vehicle. It is fascinating to be able to get a bird's-eye view of the family jitney in motion.

"DJ, I urgently need that dentist's mirror in my en-suite bathroom cabinet. Could you get it for me, right away?" the girl asks.

As they overtake the SUV, and, while the folks are still immediately above their family truck, Lyndsey slowly rotates the *System* until it completes a full one-hundred-and-eighty-degree turn.

Carefully, she backs off from the vehicle's hood, in the direction of travel, so that the family can get a clear view of the front end of the car, including a high-resolution view of the perpetrator.

The man is still blithely driving along as though he has just made the perfect pinch. Not true!

As she gets into the optimum position for good photography, James returns with the requested dental mirror. "Thanks," she says, and sticks the tiny dentist's tool into the screen to use as a rear-view device; one small enough to make it hard for the perp to see.

The girl must keep in mind that she is in reverse, and cannot afford to run into another vehicle.

Fortunately, traffic is light, and drivers are generally maintaining a hefty distance between vehicles.

With the two parties now traveling south to north, as well as face-to-face, the *System* 'driver' drops down, so that the group is hovering just above the road surface.

All this while still traveling at a fair clip.

James reaches over to Ladybuck's end of the chair and retrieves his digital camera.

Just as calmly as if he is in the peace and quiet of his own home, which, of course, he is, he kneels in front of the HDTV and takes two photographs, and approximately ten seconds of video footage of the bad guy.

His dad suggests, very reasonably, that he make very sure that the vehicle's State of Florida license tag is legible in the 'mug shots.'

Finally, she pulls over to drive above the grass-strip median, reverting to the front view before heading in the direction of home.

Buckminster, "What district attorney could refuse to prosecute this guy on the strength of this evidence? That'll teach him not to mess around with us."

"Listen, kids. It'll be a while before we get our wheels back.

"We still need the emergency generator and the UPS gear and the extra TV. Mom and I will get a taxi so that we can take the camera over to the police station on First Avenue North, over by Tropicana Field.

"We'll drop your camera off with them, James, and sign out a complaint against this bozo."

"After that, we'll truck on over to the Electronics Superstore on Route 19 North, and pick up the stuff we need.

"I'll rent one of the Superstore's pickups to bring the stuff home, or, perhaps they'll deliver it for us; it's going to be a fair-sized order."

"Russell, would it be okay if your mom and I came to the store with you?" Buck inquires.

"Sure, Dad. We'd love to have you along."

Dianne, "Remember, you two, be careful with that *System*. You're the only kids we have!"

James, "Don't forget I want my camera back in one piece!"

#

"I suppose you realize, Lynz, we could have teleported the camera over to the police department?"

"There's no such thing as teleportation," she asserts in return.

"Well, just think about Nowra. Gramps just teleported my camera from St. Petersburg to *Albatross*, where he took pictures of the S-2 Tracker, and then teleported it back here again.

"We could just as easily have gotten off the I-275, turned around and gone straight over to 1300 First Avenue North and dropped the camera off with the Desk Sergeant at the police station without bothering to drag it over there from here."

"Don't mention that in front of Dad."

"Why not, for Pete's sake?"

"Just think about it. He's a transportation specialist! Can you imagine hundreds of tanker-trailers of gasoline driving up to our house, to get their hoses into our *System* and through to filling stations in Chicago every day?

"That's just for one city, never mind every other city, town, and village in the country. The things he couldn't get up to with this portal simply aren't worth mentioning.

"Given the opportunity, everyone in the United States would be transporting themselves through a TV. Nobody would need to fly with a commercial airline any more.

"As a matter of fact, if everyone in the United States had a television set with these capabilities, every last one of President Eisenhower's interstates could close down; who'd need them any more?"

"You mean that he would have, like, Jed and Granny Clampett, Jethro and Elly May all coming through our house to get out west?"

"Sure. That old truck, and the rocker, and all."

"Yes!"

"Ouch!"

####

5 "Buenos Dias, Chris"

Two adventurous teenagers and one HDTV hooked up to the *System* make for interesting times.

It is still the afternoon of Sunday, February 22.

Mom, Dad, and the paternal grandparents are out at the police department with James' digital camera, and its flawless evidence against the car thief.

They are also destined for the electronics store, to purchase the equipment the family needs to protect the *System* from power outages.

On the kitchen TV, Lyndsey catches an NNN headline, which proclaims: A female teenager reported kidnaped almost six months ago has been found locked in a hidden room in a Toronto residence less than 300 meters from her parents' home.

The full report that follows presents the fine detail of the incident: Fourteen-year-old Lilian Dela Cruz, who was reported abducted in mid-summer, 2014, paradoxically has been found alive and well in a residence near her own home in suburban Toronto, Canada.

Better known as Lily, the popular youngster was about to embark on her very first semester at Applewood High School in Mississauga, Ontario, Toronto's twin city.

Her Labor Day disappearance, September 1, 2014, because of its occurrence on a public holiday in both Canada and the United States, was widely reported on in the media of both countries.

Although police had deemed an 'AMBER-Alert' desirable at the time, no alert was ever issued.

Part of the criteria for an Alert is the availability of a description of the abductor or a description of his vehicle, including, if possible, its license plate or tag number.

That data was simply unavailable, as the kidnaper had apparently committed his crime without a single known witness.

Despite this, more than one hundred and forty leads were telephoned or texted to official hotlines, or to Crime Stoppers.

Not one proved fruitful, despite each tip being diligently followed up by trained investigators. Most proved to be cases of mistaken identity, while not a few were later classified as hoaxes.

One report (which has now proven to be a case of mistaken identity), was texted to Crime Stoppers, stating that the youngster had been seen walking east on the Lakeshore in Toronto.

The witness reported that she had looked away for a moment or two

When she looked again, the student had vanished.

The witness could only recall seeing a young man riding a bicycle toward Etobicoke Creek in the direction of the Mississauga city line.

This generated the suspicion that the abductor might be a male.

In the update to the case, the network reports: *Officers, executing a search warrant at a house some two hundred meters from the Dela Cruz family home, reportedly found the teenager in an under-floor room.*

The warrant, issued by a judge on an unrelated matter, was to permit officials to search the premises. They were seeking merchandise stole in a number of recent robberies in the general vicinity of the perpetrator's 43rd Street home.

A police representative reported that a colleague had been 'intrigued by a squeaking floorboard.' When the source of the noise was investigated, the offending plank was found to be part of a well-concealed trapdoor, which formed an entrance to the room where the teen was being held captive.

Upon entry to the hidden chamber, the girl was found. She was handcuffed to the metal headboard of a small bed. The stolen merchandise was located in the same part of the house.

As to the girl herself, it was reported: The now-14-year-old appears to be in good shape. She reports to officials that she was allowed full bathroom privileges and given permission to take daily showers.

The criminals provided her with several changes of clothing over the early part of her confinement, allowing her to launder her clothes frequently.

Her instructions from them had included a requirement to clean her quarters at least twice each week.

Unusually, for such a case, she advised police that she not been abused by her captors. She said they appeared to be more interested in the likelihood that her father would pay the $500,000 ransom they had demanded.

Finally, the report concludes: At this time, it is not known if any arrangement has been made to pay the ransom. In the months since the kidnaping, it was felt that the Dela Cruz family would have had great difficulty in raising such a sum.

Official reports indicate that the family's neighbors are well-to-do industrialists whose children might have been the real targets of the kidnapers.

The three men found in the home at the time of the discovery of the girl have all been arrested, and are to be charged with the kidnaping tomorrow morning, February 23.

#

"Deej," Lyndsey comments, "you know, the *System* would let us solve abductions like this before the perpetrators have had time to pick up their mobile phone and order a pizza for dinner."

"You're probably right about that, Lynz," DJ allows, "but there is only one *System*, and we cannot stop crime entirely.

"Good intentions aren't much help. What we need is about a hundred of these sets, and a couple of thoroughly honest individuals to operate each one.

"I tend to think that family finances are not going to stretch that far, so we're going to have to make do with what we have for now."

"Yeah, I guess I already knew the answer to that. What I'm hoping is that we can zip off to Toronto, and use this as an experiment in how to go about using the portal to solve crimes like this.

"We could 'drive' to Mississauga and check out the girl just before she was abducted; find out who took her, and to what address.

"We can look all around the inside of the house to find the exact room in which she's being held.

"Any information we can locate that the police would be interested in, we can give them. What do you think?"

"That would involve traveling about twelve hundred miles, and about six months into the past.

"That's a whole lot shorter than the trip we did to Nowra, so we should be able to manage that without any great difficulty," the young boy replies.

"OK. That sounds about right for our test protocols."

"Can we start now?" she inquires. "But, DJ, you'll have to be careful, and not do anything foolhardy, because, don't forget, Dad said not to!"

"No, Sis. What Dad said was 'Be careful with it and don't go into the screen for anything.'"

"Deej, you're going to be a lawyer when your schooling is finished. I can smell it coming!"

James notes, "I suppose there's really no rush about this; the girl has already been rescued and we know she wasn't hurt. That will let us go about it slowly, and take our time over the details.

"We're not going to get into situations where we have to make decisions about changing history in any way, or getting to bring someone back to life.

"So this sounds like a good opportunity to set up Florida's first 'Mr. Nice Guy' service for the saving of young maidens in distress.

"Lynz, could you check out the Internet and print us a map of the border area between Toronto, and Mississauga, Ontario?" he requests. "You had better pay special attention to the area around the street and house number where the girl's family lives.

"Finally, we may need an overall view of the eastern end of Lake Ontario."

With Lynz 'driving,' the first priority is to synchronize the journal's clock with the horloge on the house wall.

Next, the siblings must adjust the view of the *Herald*'s display until it reads twelve noon on August 31, 2014. This will now match with midday on the day prior to the kidnaping at their destination.

Then the young pair slips quietly out of St. Pete's and heads due north. As agreed, there is no rush about the assignment, so Lyndsey keeps the speed to a mere blast, and it takes less than twenty seconds to get to within sight of the smallest of the five Great Lakes.

It is a thrill to get their first-ever glimpse of the 'honeymoon capital of the world,' as they pass Niagara Falls which marks the U.S./Canada border where New York State and the Canadian province of Ontario meet on the Niagara peninsula. Mississauga, Ontario, Canada, is now only about forty miles away, as the crow flies.

Once across the lake, she 'cruises' into Mississauga at Lakeshore Road East and Dixie Road.

"Look, Deej. Two golf courses; one each side of Dixie Road; we could set down on one of those and get our bearings."

"Actually, you can just stop right here in mid-air and we can get the coordinates while we're enjoying a bird's-eye view."

"Sorry, I forgot," she apologizes.

"Lynz, what do you have on this young girl? I'm looking for a home address, if you were able to get one."

"The info I found on NNN's Web site was pretty much everything we need.

"The home address I have is 1517 Lakeshore Road East. The mapping program says it's just east of Dixie Road, so we're pretty much right on the spot. I'll try 'driving' east along Lakeshore, and we'll keep an eye out for the number."

"There the numbers are, 1485 … 1489 … 1493, … then a gap and … 1517. OK, here we are, Lynz.

"Now, drive along the path leading up to the front door.

"No action here, Lynz, which means that the girl is still OK for now.

"Say, did you get a photograph of the girl off the Web site?"

"It's in that folder on the sofa next to you."

"Got it; thanks.

"Are you positioned so as to be fairly low-profile, Lynz? We can't afford to have anyone spot us?"

"Probably, but I could take us over beside that hedge, and snuggle in on the north side of it, so that spotting us will be a lot more difficult."

"That's a good idea. Once you get us there, could you then move us ahead a few hours, maybe ten or twelve in small increments, say of about one hour, until we start to see a whole bunch of police cars running around?

"I'm sticking my watch back outside, so we can keep track of the time back in last August and September. It's adjusted to show the same date and time as the *Sunshine-Herald.*

"Once you see the boys in blue in their squad cars, you can put it in reverse, and, after that, we'll just keep an eye open for the girl and the bad guy."

Lyndsey acts as requested.

"Zip, and what do you know, the cops have already shown up. That's cool! Now back-up in increments of roughly one half-an-hour."

"Slow down, Deej. Don't forget I have to keep eyeballing the watch to make the changes of time, otherwise we're not able to keep track of what the exact time is."

"There's the first one, DJ."

"What time was that on the watch?" the boy asks.

"3:00 p.m.," the older sibling responds. "Although Mississauga and St. Pete's are both in the same time zone, it's handy that we don't have to dart back and forth to check the journal's time.

"I'm so glad Mom came up with the idea of using your old watch," Lynz remarks.

"Another hour, please; there are still cops at the house."

"OK, that's 2:00 p.m. now," she reports.

"Good. All the cops have vanished; meaning they haven't shown up yet ... Hey, it says on the hard copy of the NNN webpage, that Lily was taken at about 12:45 p.m., just after noon on Labor Day, but that she actually left from the back door of her home.

"We'd better zip around the rear door, and then pedal backward until the watch shows 12:30 p.m., and then just creep forward until the perpetrator shows up and the incident takes place."

"Round to the back; then reverse in time to 12:30 p.m. Done, Captain!

"You asked for small movements in a forward direction, DJ, so I'm moving forward in time one click at a time."

#

"There's someone coming, Lynz! The door's opening."

The girl thinks to herself, "Hmm ... Accurate prophecy, James. The girl is just coming out. The NNN picture is excellent; it's easy to see it's her."

"LP, ease the *System* up in the air so that we can watch Lily and see where she goes and who she talks to.

"By the way, what's the exact time?"

"1:36 p.m."

"Thanks. I'm making a note of that for our records."

Lilian, dressed in blue jeans and a dark blue top, strolls along the north side of Lakeshore Road in an easterly direction, toward the nearby Long Branch bus station of the Toronto Transit Commission.

Her home is beside the Mississauga/Toronto boundary, marked by the waters of Etobicoke Creek.

The Florida siblings follow her every step with the greatest of interest.

Less than seventy-five paces beyond Etobicoke Creek, she comes to Forty-third Street, Etobicoke, a part of metropolitan Toronto, an L-shaped cul-de-sac having four small, three-story apartment buildings and eight single-family dwellings.

As she passes along the Lakeshore beside the southernmost apartment block, a young man exits from the side door of the building.

As he sees Lilian, he quickly sizes her up, and then ducks to take advantage of the cover of the building's bushes. The soon-to-be high-school student sees nothing of this.

It takes but a second to approach her; cupping his hand over her mouth to prevent her from screaming, he takes her by the wrist and, with a quick glance around to make sure he hasn't been spotted, he drags the student into the bushes.

Thanks to the old chrono, DJ is quickly able to note that it is 1:44 p.m.

The youthful Toronto native changes his grip on the youngster to hold her more securely, and takes her over to the side door by which he has just exited from the apartment building, and, using a key, lets himself back in.

As he drags the girl in backward behind him, she desperately looks for a way to raise the alarm, or let someone know what is happening, but to no avail.

He continues to maintain his hand over her mouth to keep her from calling out.

Lily's abductor drags her in complete silence from the side of the edifice right through to the rear of the structure, where he uses a 'panic bar' to exit via the back door.

His next move is to take her from the rear of the apartment building, and, when the coast is clear, he guides her into one of the westernmost houses across the L-shaped street, at 1455 Forty-third Street.

Letting himself in at the side door of the house, he slams the door behind the girl to make sure that the lock positively engages.

A position as assistant superintendent for all four apartment buildings gives him easy access to the facility, as well as proximity to his home.

He is totally unaware, of course, of the presence of the dynamic Richardson duo, now in hot pursuit. The *System* has already 'penetrated' cleanly through the apartment block in close proximity to the bad guy and his kidnap victim.

Lyndsey has no need of a key for the lock. She simply 'intrudes' the residence by way of the rear of the house, to avoid arousing any alarm on the man's part.

She simply 'drives' from room to room until she finds the perpetrator on the ground floor.

As he holds Lilian Dela Cruz in a tight grip and, with his single free hand, applies duct tape to her mouth to prevent her screams.

He handcuffs her to a hot-water radiator, to keep her securely attached to the building.

It is early September; the heating device is not in use. There is no fear of Lily being burned by the unit.

James is easily able to get photographs of both a full face and a profile of the man, just in case.

The kids are not going to attempt a rescue, since Lily is, in reality, already freed by Toronto police.

But, from the present standpoint, this will not be until next February, when the police discover the young girl during their search for property stolen from the apartment buildings.

The owners of the four multi-family buildings had on several occasions reported to authorities the theft of valuable electrical and electronic tools from the basement workshop.

The police already had 'probable cause' against the suspect, so they applied for a warrant from a judge. This is received, and executed.

During their search of the home, officers stumble over the captive lass.

This whole matter is already 'history,' so to speak, and the duo is checking it out simply as an exercise in feasibility, to see if they could do this all over again.

Next time, it will likely be a genuine AMBER-Alert situation, meaning a young child has been kidnaped and has not been found.

The experience they are gaining on this expedition will be invaluable next time around.

Now Lyndsey moves ahead in time until the perp opens the trapdoor to the hidden room in which Lilian Dela Cruz will be discovered in several months.

Only when the young kidnap victim has been transferred into the holding chamber, and securely handcuffed to the headboard, does Lyndsey penetrate the floorboards.

DJ is busy too, and obtains photos and video of the whole scene to solidify the evidence against the villain.

James' DVD writer continues to capture valuable footage of everything that transpires through the screen.

The *System* 'intrudes' the 'cell,' and descends to the level of the ceiling fan, so that Lynz and DJ are able to look down upon the girl, as she lies sobbing on the bed.

James, from the former comfort of the now-wrecked sofa in their family room, takes three photos and brief video of Lily.

There will be no value in assuring her that 'eventually' she will be rescued, so Lyndsey 'elevates' the *System* completely out of the house by way of the roof and heads for the front door.

Upon arrival at the main entrance, Deej makes a video record of the house number, 1455, as well as a view of the house and street.

Lyndsey 'drives' over to the street sign and her brother makes a brief video of the sign as well as an overall view of the area.

"You know," he says, "that whole operation only took us about thirty minutes once Lily was in that guy's control. If we had been able to go to the police for information, we probably could have done the whole thing in even less."

"Listen, is that enough excitement for one day, or would you want to think about going somewhere else while we're waiting for Dad and Mom?"

"Don't forget Dad's instruction, DJ. It's still valid."

"I didn't go out when we were working in Mississauga, did I?"

"That's true; you even stayed this side of the portal when you were taking your pictures and video.

"Remember, though, if you're dead, exactly who gets to carry the can back? Mois, mon frère, mois ..." the girl says as she DELTAs her way back to the Florida newspaper.

"So, where would you like to go today, madam?"

Deej, in response to his own question, "How about '1-4-9-2' and ENTER."

As he speaks, the boy changes video disks in the DVD burner.

"1492? Are you kidding?

"Alright, '1-4-9-2' plus ENTER. DJ, it's a forest … nothing else."

"It's a forest alright … but which forest? … Think about it for a second … Remember what we had through the screen before we started out?"

"Good grief, Deej. This is the property the *Sunshine-Herald* will build its offices on … in about … three hundred and fifty years!"

"Great. Now try this on for size. Say we key ahead in time to October of the year 1492, elevate ourselves to about 3,000 feet, then 'cruise' out toward the Caribbean, perhaps past Miami, or, at least, where Miami will be in a few hundred years."

"After that, we could make a ninety-degree turn east over the Atlantic Ocean, stop, then advance in time, and watch out for three ships sailing in formation."

"Do you mean the *Niña*, the *Pinta*, and the *Santa Maria*? How do you know when they sailed?"

"A lecture we had last week on American history from Mr. Bonofiglio included the date of September 6, 1492, when Christopher Columbus sailed from the Canary Islands; his only stop on the way to the Americas.

"Mr. B. cited a trip lasting about four weeks. That time span would be up in early- to mid-October.

"The *System* defaults to the beginning of the year; so if we nominate 1492 as our destination year, we'll automatically wind up at January first.

"After that, we'll need to do the old watch on the coat hanger trick outside the portal again, so that I can start advancing to October, 1492.

"That will save us having to go count the number of days, because we have no way to know the actual date or time out here."

"Hold on a second; why don't we try it out without the modern technology ... That's quite a compliment for your old chronometer, by the way.

"Remember how you did it with Pyle's memorial on Ie Shima? You asked the big sergeant to give you the date. That worked okay. Let's try that again, just to see if we can work out the answer to this question of five hundred years ago."

"What do you want to do, stop a ship and ask somebody?"

"I can't believe you said that!" Lyndsey explodes.

"It's actually not such a bad idea as you might think. Every ship has a log of some kind, even back then, and the date would be part of the information that they recorded each day, if the crew was to keep proper track of the voyage."

"Listen, since we are able to travel at high speed, is there somewhere we could take the *System* to find out what the date is? Like, maybe, London?"

"Perhaps we could find a poster or sign that has a date on it. There were no newspapers back in those days."

"Hey, not bad!" the boy banters.

"A compass and a map would be handy if we're going to be out in the middle of nowhere during the Middle Ages. Do you want to get them from Dad's office?"

The boy leaves his sibling in charge of the touch-pad device while he walks toward the back of the house and steps into his dad's workplace.

He checks for the world map that he knows Russell keeps in his desk. He picks up his dad's compass, and, "I guess Dad's binoculars might be handy too!"

#

"Thanks, Deej. Before you start though, how about putting your watch outside anyway, and we'll use it to verify the information, so that we're not getting misled about the actual date we've arrived at."

Lyndsey opts to DELTA back once more to the journal's office, and adjust the date and time to match that displayed in the rec room.

James adjusts the date on his old digital watch to match the other media, and then hangs it on the coat hanger outside their 2015 time machine.

Lyndsey returns to the heavily forested view of St. Petersburg, whereupon DJ verified that the company watch is displaying January 1, 1492, as it should.

"Try moving forward in time and gently holding the key down, for about half a second. We need to move forward about six or seven months, to get closer to the date we're looking for," he directs.

Slowly, they worked their way forward to about the middle of summer according to the position of the sun at noon.

"OK. Right now," he tells her, tracing a line of latitude on the map with his finger, "we need to travel this way across the Atlantic to go to London, which is just here, roughly east of our present position.

"Try going that way and elevate us up to 3,000 feet, and we should be able to see the British Isles fairly quickly."

"Where did you have in mind to go to get the date, Lynz?"

"Well, back in the 1490s, people were not making a big deal about counting time the way we do today. It just didn't seem that important to them.

"Folks pretty much calculated the days and years based on how long it was since the lord of the manor died, or when the barn burned down.

"Newspapers will not show up for a couple of hundred years, so I figure we'll have to go to some place where they will definitely have the date sorted out for themselves."

"Such as? … Big Ben? ... Sorry, it was supposed to be a joke."

"We would probably have to go somewhere like the home of the King of England. His guards are sure to have the info we need."

"You mean, like, Buckingham Palace? What makes you think someone there will have an idea what the date is?"

"I'll have to research this, but it's very possible that 'The Palace' doesn't exist back in 1492, and the King made his home somewhere else." The girl reached for her mobile.

"I figure that a gatekeeper is sure to know the date.

"If he's anything like other soldiers, he's using a calendar of some kind and is keeping track day-by-day of how long it is till he gets out of the service!"

#

"Look at this, Deej."

"What did you find? I've been waiting for you to finish with the Internet.

"We're sitting off the south coast of England. That's the Isle of Wight just over there, and beyond it is the city of Southampton."

"Well, Buckingham Palace was a good idea, but it won't wash, I'm afraid."

"Whaddya mean?"

"Well, it seems the palace wasn't even built until 1703, and didn't come into use as the official royal residence until the middle of the nineteenth century, the 1830s, that is; during Queen Victoria's reign," she reports.

"So, that leaves us two choices: 1) The Tower of London, or, 2) Windsor Castle.

"Both of these were in use as family residences by the royals since the ten hundreds, just after the Battle of Hastings in 1066 CE."

"Here's something to think about, What kind of people are we going to visit? I think the Tower of London wasn't just the home of the monarch of the time."

From their history classes, both are aware that the Royal Family back then is not made up of the royals that we know today.

Five hundred and twenty-three years ago is seven years into the reign of the first sovereign ruler of the Tudor Dynasty, King Henry VII.

Too, they are not all nice people; the King's son is just about one year old. On April 22, 1509, he will become England's most infamous king, Henry VIII.

"Another item, although it doesn't really affect our visit, The old world is still using the Julian calendar, but, like I said, that's pretty much insignificant.

"If someone is able to give us the date, they'll be giving us the information based on that same calendar."

"Are you all set to head on in to the Tower?"

"Sure; when you're ready."

"OK, go ahead; but just be certain you approach the building slowly. We need to make sure we're not getting into something we can't handle."

"London on the starboard beam, Cap'n," she calls out, mimicking old-time sailors.

"OK, keep going as you are, toward the center of the city. There! You can see the bends in the River Thames; just follow those.

"We actually passed Windsor Castle about ten kilometers back, on the way into town. It's a much quieter area than the city, and so because of the hustle and bustle of the big city, we're more likely to get a response here in the city of London.

"See the Tower? It's the biggest building around."

"Got it! I'll circle it first, just to be sure."

"Looks like you're right. There are guards on duty outside. Gosh, what scruffy uniforms!"

"Henry VII probably can't afford anything better; they're just over the War of the Roses a few years back. He likely spent all his money fighting that conflict."

"There's a guard all alone, over there by the big lawn."

"Here goes!"

Deej calls out, "Excuse me, sir."

"Pray tell me how I can help thee, young master."

"Wow! Thanks, sir ... Could you please tell me what the date is on your calendar today?"

"Why, of course; it's just thirty days since the birth of the King's daughter, the Princess Elizabeth. Today it be the first day of August, Anno Domini 1492."

"May I please inquire as to your name, sir?"

"Aye, John of Pytchley, East Anglia, young sir."

"Have you a family name, sir?"

"Aye, master. Of the family Summerfield, of Lower End, Pytchley."

"Master, the bench upon which thine companion art seated; what becometh of it?"

"Thank you kindly for asking, John Summerfield of Pytchley, but it's a long story, sir, and we have to bid you good-day."

"Have thyself a good day, nay, thee both."

Lynz 'drives' away from the Tower of London, grateful that her head is still attached, unlike that of many another visitor to this same venue.

"Hold it, Lynz! Look at the name of that street close to the Tower. 'Pudding Lane!' Holy cow! The king should have someone set up a few 'No Smoking' signs. That's where the Great Fire of London will start in 174 years, in 1666."

"Impressive, Deej. John Summerfield's date agrees exactly with your watch; August 1.

"Now I can press the DELTA button to get us back out to the western Atlantic, and do the time travel routine until Chris shows up with his water-buses.

"What a helpful man John Summerfield was. His family must be very proud of him; being in the service of the King, and all."

"OK, Deej. Now we are back near mid-ocean … finally onto a western heading … advancing in time. Keep your eye on the watch from here on in.

"John Summerfield of East Anglia told us that it was August first. How are we doing on the watch?"

#

"Hold it there with the higher-speed stuff, Lynz. Slow it down to a jog for now.

"The watch is showing October 1, so we probably need to move a little closer to the mainland, or at least the Caribbean area, if we're going to find the three ships; they'll be landing in a few days.

"Maybe, too, we should continue to about three thousand feet, and cruise over toward the island of Hispaniola." Lyndsey complies smoothly.

"Once we get there, we'll need to keep a sharp lookout for three smallish sailing ships.

"Officially, *Niña*, and *Pinta*, the swiftest of the three, are of the caravel type, about sixty feet long. *Niña* is a three-master, while *Pinta* has two or three masts, and both are square-rigged.

"*Santa Maria* is of the carrack type and carries three masts. In length, she would be about eighty-two feet long.

"Weight-wise, they run around fifty tons and each carries a crew of only twenty-five to forty men, so they're not big ships, by any means."

#

"There are three lights in formation, DJ. It's too dim to see, but if I 'nudge' the *System* and 'edge' it forward a couple of hours, it will turn into daylight."

#

"There, now we can see that it's a formation of three sailing ships … Still traveling together … Near to Hispaniola … They're heading north though, not west … Maybe it's not him.

"I'll zip in and have a quick look.

"Hey. They look about the right size, DJ, and they appear to be together."

"*Buenos dias, señor.*"

Now his Spanish-language classes really pay off in spades.

"Excuse me, *señor.*" Ever the polite one, the youngster continues in the mother tongue of the person who appears to be in charge of the crewmembers on deck.

"Might I inquire if these are the vessels of Christopher Columbus, sailing in the name of Her Royal Majesty Queen Isabella of Spain?"

"They are, sir. And may I inquire as to who wishes to know this?"

"We are travelers familiar with this area. Hopefully, we can provide some assistance should you require it."

"Our leader hoped to find land here, but we are running low on provisions and water.

"We are going to have to abandon our search soon, if we don't find it.

"May I bring our leader to the deck, so that you may reassure him?"

"Por supuesto, señor."

The officer calls one of his men and issues him a brusque command and the sailor hurries off toward the fo'c'sle) of the vessel.

Moments later, a red-haired man emerges from the superstructure and walks confidently over to the officer the teens had first addressed.

"*Buon giorno, signor. Buenos dias, señor.*"

James greets the then little-known explorer in both his native Italian, and also in the language of his adopted Spain.

He feels a deep sense of relief that he had listened attentively when his homeroom teacher, Mr. Bonofiglio, was explaining greetings in the Italian language.

His use of the Spanish language continues, so as not to exclude the subordinate from the conversation.

"*Señor*, my companion and I are very familiar with the area in which you are now sailing.

"Your executive officer has indicated to us that you would be appreciative of assistance that would help you to find the land you have been seeking.

"Would you be willing to accept a suggestion that would help you to bring your voyage to a successful conclusion?"

"*Señor*, your assistance would be very welcome. Her Majesty Queen Isabella and her husband Ferdinand would also be most grateful. What assistance are you able to render?"

James now ponders exactly how to word his directions to Christopher Columbus. He feels a need to make it simple, while maintaining a professional appearance as he is dealing with a man who will, one day, be highly respected in his field.

"*Señor*," he says, reaching out for Russell's compass, "this is the compass of my father. As you can see, it indicates that you are traveling from south to north. The land you seek is …"

Lyndsey leans over to James on the sofa and urgently whispers to him, "James! Tell Mr. Columbus to follow those birds just passing above the ships; they're heading west.

"He needs to change direction and go west, if they're ever going to find anything. Those birds are American Golden Plovers, and a flock of Eskimo Curlews just flew over ahead of the plovers.

"Tell him they are shore birds, and to go in that direction; they're flying toward land. That'll get him where he's going!"

" … just a little further west of our present location, *Señor*.

"In verification of that, Excellency, my companion has identified those birds overhead as land birds and they are flying to their homes.

"Follow them, and they will lead you to the land of plenty that is just over the horizon to the west."

"You are so kind, *señor*."

"It's our pleasure, *señor*."

"Before I depart, *señor*, may I ask a question?"

"Of course!"

"The bench upon which your companion is seated; what happened to it?"

"It's a long story, but thank you for asking, *señor*. *Gracias y hasta la vista, mi amigo*."

"*Nuestro placer, Señor*."

"*Muchas gracias, Señor*," the grateful Columbus responds.

"*Nuestro placer, Señor*." James maintains his decorum to the end.

Columbus communicates the information to his helmsman, and the three ships vector slowly to the west, and then move toward the horizon.

To the west, this time, not the north, as they had been sailing previously.

"Great," James thinks. "Lynz comes through with her bird stuff again!"

#

"Hi Mom, Hi Dad!"

"Hey, guys; watcha been up to while we were out?"

"Oh, nothing much; just gave some directions to some guys who were lost."

"Like, what were they looking for?"

"They were trying to find America."

"Say what?"

"DELTA, Lynz."

"Done. 'DELTA.' Presto! Guys looking for America, back in October, 1492!"

"Is that Christopher Columbus? The three sailing ships; are they the *Niña*, the *Pinta*, and the *Santa Maria*?

"Holy cow, guys. What on earth did you tell them?"

"How to find America … or at least we pointed them west, rather then the direction in which they were traveling, north.

"Dad, Mom, this was beautiful. Lynz blinded them with her birdie-science and we sent them off toward Hispaniola."

"Well, at least we can be sure that our homeland will be discovered one of these years. That's reassuring."

"Did you get any pictures?"

"Naturally!"

#

"OK, fellas; Mom and I bought the stuff we went out for; and we filed the complaint against that idiot who pinched our SUV.

"You know, Deej, the Desk Sergeant looked at your camera and he just laughed. Seems the joker has a season ticket to the local hoosegow. His name is Carlos Gonzales.

"The 'sarge' said it's the best evidence against a car thief he's ever seen.

"He was a little curious as to how we got the footage and the pictures.

"We just laughed and explained that we just happened to be in the neighborhood with a camera."

"Actually, I asked him if he would be interested in a service that provides footage like that."

"And…?"

"Well, he said that any police department in the country that decided to pass on a service like that would be nuts! Stealing cars would become as extinct as the Dodo bird."

"So, what's with the two boxes?"

"Boy, I'd forgotten them already. The generator weighed over 100 pounds, so we left it for the Superstore to deliver tomorrow. They promised it would be here before 10:00 a.m.

"The other boxes are the second TV and the UPS equipment. They were fairly light, so we decided we could manage those OK … we took a taxi home for the four of us."

"We dropped Grandma and Gramps off at home on the way here. They'll be back tomorrow morning."

"The *System* is costing us a pretty penny … we should start trying to make some money with it soon. It's going to have to pay for itself eventually."

"It's funny you should mention that, Dad," James responds. "This portal is extremely entertaining, and, like with the car thief, we can get some use out of it, too."

"True, but that's expensive entertainment. This isn't just like any other TV.

"If you switch a regular TV off, you can turn it on again; this one has to have all sorts of expensive gadgetry to keep it going and you can never turn it off, at least not that we know of, so far."

"Dad, what would be the possibility of delivering small packages to people anywhere in the world? For a fee, naturally.

"That would generate good income for the *System*, and we would be able to cover the cost of the electronic back-up equipment we have to maintain."

"James!"

"Dad, Lyndsey doesn't want me to mention it to you, but did you know that this *System* will allow us to teleport things?"

Dad replies, "What?"

"Well, like I told Lyndsey, Granddad teleported my digital camera to Okinawa. He took a picture of Mr. Pyle's grave marker, and then teleported the camera back to St. Pete's.

"My idea was that we could offer ... like ... a courier service, for people who want to send letters and envelopes.

"Stuff that is so urgent that they have to have it delivered right away, by hand."

"Say, as an example, the president, in Washington, wants to send a private note, or something like that, over to the government in England.

"We could take it for him, many times faster than a jet fighter could, and can teleport it from his door at 1600 Pennsylvania Avenue, to the prime minister's door at 10 Downing Street in London.

"Door to door in minutes! Seconds, even, when we get the hang of it a little more … Some extra practice with the controls.

"Gosh, I hope the *System* never packs it in on us."

"Can you plug in this uninterruptible power source unit for me, James?"

"Hold on, Dad. How can you plug the TV into the UPS equipment without unplugging it from the wall receptacle first?"

"Good grief. This is a bit beyond my electrical and electronic capabilities. I never thought of that.

"Of course, to plug the *System* into the UPS, we first have to disconnect it from the house supply.

"It's a good thing one of us is thinking today.

"We have to find someone to wire the *System* with a second plug, without disconnecting it of course, so that it can be looped into the house supply and the UPS at the same time.

"Then, if there is a power cut, the UPS can fill the power needs until the electricity comes back on.

"Ultimately, we'll need to plug the *System* into the generator, as it will be connected to the house supply and when the main power fails the generator will fill in for most of the building, including the *System*.

"I sure hope that this makes electrical sense."

"How can we get the electrician to do this work without him seeing what's on the *System*?" James queries.

"We'll just have to tell him that we're recording a special program with our DVD-writer and hope he believes us.

"Incidentally, this power problem won't arise with the new TV Mom and I bought.

"It's a smaller version of the plasma-screen HDTV, just the same as the big one here, but it's equipped with a built-in battery back-up, so, a power cut can't hurt us.

"You can't do anything with the big set until the re-wiring gets done, so can I get Lynz to give me a hand to set up the new TV right here?"

"By all means."

#

"Hey, Dad! The new TV's ready to go; do you want to come and watch while Lyndsey plugs it in?"

"On the way!" The adults come down for the big event.

"OK! NNN, at last! I was beginning to have withdrawal symptoms. I thought I'd never see John Rocks again."

"Dad, it's John Cox ... not John Rocks!"

Russell gasps, "Wow ... what's been going on in the world? ... It seems like weeks since I last saw the news."

"You know there are sure to be three wars, four murders, fifteen robberies, and, if it is John Cox, then our southern border is bound to be flooded with illegal immigrants. What else is new?"

"OK, James, if we're going to take a crack at something on the *System*, then perhaps you can move the new TV over next to the big one. OK?

"You can plug it into that receptacle just there." He points to one about nine feet to the right of the original large-screen TV.

"Thanks, son."

Dianne asks, "Can I choose somewhere to take us one of these days?"

"Such as, Di?"

"Windsor Castle."

"Yes, ma'am."

"We could even watch out for 10 Downing Street on the way past."

"Deej!"

"Sorry."

####

6 Paw Paw's Big Secret

"Kids, we've got to make some changes.

"What James discovered has already caused to us make huge adjustments in our lives, but we cannot just ignore this phenomenon, nor can we abandon our normal way of life.

"This strange effect we are seeing on the HDTV is going to make us go about our lives in a different way.

"You two haven't missed much school yet, which is good. We have to avoid doing anything that could cause you to lose any advantage you have in your schoolwork.

"Your mom's family probably thinks she has fallen off the edge of the earth; it's very abnormal for them not to hear from her just about every day.

"I haven't touched anything in my office since the *System* turned up. Too, there are things that we have to care for around the house.

"Although there is a need for all of us to get back to our regular routine, we must acknowledge the incredible gift we've been given, and try to build our lives around this portal, at least for as long as we have it available to us."

"What are you thinking of, Dad? What will we do with the *System*?"

"Listen. One extremely crucial thing to remember is that it's important that we not tell a soul about what's happened to the TV. Do you understand that?

"You were right in what you said the other day, DJ. We have to make every effort to keep this inside the family circle, just for our own 'peace and security.'"

"We have to plan carefully for the time that we will need to let someone know about it, but when, though, is another story.

"Remember those old World War II posters we saw? 'Even walls have ears,' and, 'Loose lips sink ships.' No one finds out until we're good and ready. Do you understand that, Lyndsey?"

"Yes, I guess that does make a lot of sense."

"James?"

"OK, Dad; you can count on both of us, for sure."

"Then, we can experiment with it in the evenings."

#

"When will we get our SUV back from the police, Dad?"

"I called the desk sergeant today and he said that when the thief saw the video evidence against him, he pled guilty.

"The sarge says that means they won't have to hold our car while they search it for evidence, and, hopefully, it should be back to us no later than this time tomorrow."

Dianne, "So I'll be able to get to the market then. That's good. I've got food enough for all of us for a pot-luck dinner tonight."

#

Next day, the siblings are back in high school, and Dianne is again at the routine of the household.

Russell is once more trying to be a transportation specialist, although, left to his own devices, just like the others, he is giving extraordinary thought to things to do with *System*.

He is not concerned so much for financial advantage. Rather, he's considering different things to experiment with so that the family will be able to get the very best use out of it.

Especially he thinks that, if there is some way in which all of humankind could benefit from this phenomenon, and then this should govern the avenue of experimentation that is pursued.

"I suppose the commercial possibilities are endless.

"Think about it … This is mind-boggling! … Who would ever need to fly with a commercial airline again?

"Who would need to drive anywhere? … Anyone with a television hooked up to the *System* who wants to visit his or her granny in Poughkeepsie, NY, only has to climb into his or her TV.

"If gasoline gets too expensive I suppose one could always nuke oneself back to Chicago, in Al Capone's days … get a few gas cans filled at 1920s prices.

"Wouldn't that be just peachy-keen! … Hee, Hee, Hee! … "Eat your heart out, Mr. Oil Company Executive!"

"Forget it! It would never work. I'd run into someone I know, and the cat would be out of the bag!"

#

Doing the laundry of the past few days, Dianne is musing to herself about the possibility of doing her grocery marketing.

Not by chauffeuring the gas-guzzling SUV, but by using the *System* to get to the market.

"It would be simple … Push the grocery cart out to the *System* 'parked' just outside the store, and unload the groceries directly into the family room.

"The kids can take them upstairs to the kitchen and laundry room … Beautiful!

"If groceries get too expensive, I can 'fly' myself back to 1910 … 105 years ago … five years before World War I, and buy food at big bucks less than everyone else pays today … I can have the best of both worlds," she daydreams.

"Forget it! It would never work. I'd run into someone I know, and the cat would be out of the bag!"

#

DJ has a history class and sits spellbound. Mr. Bonofiglio is an excellent teacher, but today, even he cannot weave his spell over James.

"... just as some of those who shared in conquering the western frontier were genuinely great heroes.

"A few, because of the good they did; others simply caught the fancy of prominent writers, like E.Z.C. Judson, whom you might know by his pen name, Ned Buntline.

"Buntline was a very prolific dime-novel writer, who latched onto the likes of Wyatt Earp, Bat Masterson, Bill Tilghman, and a couple of other deputy marshals in Dodge City of the 1870s.

"He filled his novels with stories about these men, but mostly they were tales based on mythical information with which those men had reportedly supplied.

"He praised their alleged exploits so highly, which caused these ones to rise to such repute that it made their names become legends in their own time.

"Even German and Japanese combatants from World War II cited Wild West stories and movies as a reason to be in fear of the resourcefulness and skill of American GI's during that war.

"In fact, Buntline reportedly felt extremely indebted to the Kansas lawmen.

"He is heavily rumored to have rewarded the subjects of those fantastic pursuits by commissioning the Colt's firearms factory in Hartford, Connecticut, to produce six very special 1876 Colt .45-caliber Peacemaker revolvers.

"These pistols themselves became legendary in later years, as the *Buntline Special*, through their association with these now famous ...," he mused on ... and on ... and on.

#

"One place I must go with the *System* is Tombstone, Arizona, to see the live action as it was at the O.K. Corral," DJ dreams in color.

"Better still, let me go back to Whitechapel in London in 1888, and find out who Jack the Ripper really was. The British authorities are still asking questions about that today.

"Or, maybe, I could slip over to Pearl Harbor back in 1941, to watch the Japanese raid that sank the U.S. fleet there.

"Why not go to Los Angeles a couple of decades ago, and help O.J. to find out who really did kill Nicole Brown and Ron Goldman?

"Forget it! It would never work. I'd run into someone I know, and the cat would be out of the bag!"

#

It is Geog. class for Lyndsey this morning. Mrs. Gomez is a riveting speaker and Lynz is generally a great listener, but somehow, today, Mrs. G. just isn't cutting the mustard.

"… hidden geographic features, like the Challenger Deep. This is a part of an undersea area covered with valleys, called the Marianas Trench, located close to Saipan, in the Pacific Ocean.

"That trench has been sounded to a depth of 35,838 feet. Now, that's a deep hole in anybody's language.

"Take note, too, of the tallest mountain in the world, Mount Everest. Everest was measured recently at 29,028 feet.

"Think about this, You flip Mount Everest upside-down and drop it, point down, into the Marianas Trench.

"Not only is the mountain completely covered with water, but you have almost seven thousand feet of water between the base of Mount Everest and the surface of the ocean.

"That's …," she drones on.

Well, the truth is that the body is there, but the spirit certainly is not.

"Hey," Lyndsey daydreams, "wouldn't it be neat to 'fly' over to Nepal to see Mount Everest; or maybe we could 'run' over to Kuala Lumpur and check out its skyscrapers."

"Forget it! It would never work. I'd run into someone I know, and the cat would be out of the bag!"

#

At long last! School is over; dinner on a tray, looking at the *System,* at last!

"Where shall we go?" the first addict asks.

#

Next day, Russell is out to pick up the truck. Dianne has gone with him. The catch-up marketing can be done on the way home.

Pedagogical day at school … Kids have the day to themselves; footloose and fancy-free.

"Lynz, since you're up, could you pull the new TV over a couple of feet?" Not a major assignment, since the new HDTV is on a roller table.

"Done! Why?"

"Just want to keep an eye on NNN; to see what's going on in the world. Thanks, Sis."

"OK. Here we go; daybreak in Kuala Lumpur! You can see on the skyline what you wanted to check out. The Petronas Towers, once the world's tallest buildings."

"What's with the 'once'?"

"Sorry, LP. I just checked on a couple of Web sites. Petronas Towers, in K.L., did hold the title of world's tallest buildings, but not for long.

"Then the title briefly went to Taipei 101, in, believe it or not, Taipei, Taiwan. Whaddya say we go there?"

"OK, I guess so … There are so many 'world's highest buildings' going up these days, it's hard to keep track."

"Oh, Deej, these things are fascinating … If only I could bring Mrs. Gomez."

"Ah, ah! Remember what Dad and Mom told us.

"There we are: The Taipei 101 skyscraper at sunrise. Your every wish is my command, O master," parroting the hyper-cooperative genie from Aladdin's famous lamp.

"I know, it's just that it's frustrating, having this capability at our fingertips and not being able … **Oh, no, DJ! Not again?**"

"What have I done now?"

"Not you, you twit! Look at the new TV!"

"Call Dad on his mobile and tell him what's happened! Get him to come home right away!"

"This is incredible! Why on earth is this happening?"

Staring them in the face through the small flat screen of the new HDTV is the Taipei 101 tower. It shows a miniaturized version of exactly what is currently visible on the large-screen TV.

"Move the little TV away from the *System*!"

"No difference."

"Lynz, is someone doing this to us? This has to be a gift from heaven. Perhaps we're supposed to do something with it, some good works, to show our support for God and his ways."

"It's frightening, James. You might be right, otherwise why is everything falling into place the way it is?

"First, it's one TV; then everything we try on the remote control, (once we finally figure out what it does,) starts to work in a very logical sequence.

"Then, as if that's not enough, we get a second TV which apparently works normally, but when we move it to within a couple of feet of the *System*, it starts to act in the same way.

"This has to be a gift from some superhuman power. Other people have no access to any of the things we've been seeing or doing."

"We'll just have to let Dad and Mom take a crack at answering that."

"Listen, I'll call them right away."

#

"Lyndsey! Did I hear you right on the cell phone?"

"I'm afraid so. This scares me, Dad. Why is this happening to us?

"Nobody else is able to travel in time, or go around the world in just seconds. James thinks it might be a gift from the Creator because He wants us to use it to do good works for Him."

"Wow, son, that might be stretching things a bit too far."

"Dad, it's not just me. Granddad made a rather interesting comment just before you got home from Atlanta on Saturday.

"He said everything seems to be falling into place. Every button we have pushed on the remote control has shown some desirable effect. Things like that just don't happen out of the blue.

"You won't know about him mentioning this, because you hadn't arrived home yet, but he spoke about Bartlett James trying to shoot an enemy soldier, and had eight dud cartridges out of eight.

"Remember that quote from Newton's Third Law of Motion, Dad, 'For every action, there is an equal and opposite re-action'? How does that all fit in here?

"I can't help but wonder why, suddenly, we received this fantastic capability of world and time travel, despite the fact that an operation of this kind is absolute science-fiction to everyone else on this planet."

"James, perhaps we should think about a little experiment; perhaps the way Sir Isaac Newton might have approached our problem if he had to face this situation.

"Let's unplug the small TV and let it run on its own battery. Then, take it upstairs to the living room, and see what happens."

"OK, Dad." Lyndsey volunteers, "I can do that. Call out to me and tell me what to do when I get there, though."

#

"Dad! I'm in the living room!"

"What's on the screen, Lyndsey?"

"Taipei, still!"

"Now plug it into the wall receptacle beside the dining table."

Lynz, "I've done that, Dad. It still shows Taipei."

"Unplug the set, and disconnect its battery!"

A few seconds later, "Screen's gone off!"

"Reconnect just the battery, turn it back on and tell me what comes onto the screen."

Just moments later, "NNN is back!"

"Thanks, Lyndsey! Can you please leave the set switched on, but on battery power only, and bring it back down here?

"Now, don't plug it into the house power; just set it back down on the wheelie cart.

"Bingo! That's what I thought might happen ... Taipei! ... Back to the *System*!"

Dianne, "This is scary!"

Russell, "This is taking on a rather new perspective ... and it's also becoming a 'cost-is-no-object' situation.

"I'll have to get another TV; identical to the second set so that we can check out what happens when we power down our original set.

"We must make sure that we don't lose anything. Until then, we have to keep the big-screen set running full time, just in case.

"If it works the way I think, or hope it works, maybe we can splash the idea of having the UPS wired to the big TV.

"James, 'drive' us over to Taipei 101, and set us down on the roof, if you would; I'd like to try something."

Seconds later, "Hold it there, son."

"Di! It's time you went out and took a picture or two."

"Are you joking? No cotton-pickin' way!"

"Well, I can't waste an opportunity like this!" Her husband eases his body through the large-screen TV and out into the early-morning ambience of a gorgeous Taipei day.

The flat area of the roof is very limited, but Russell found it plenty big enough for his purposes.

He takes a couple of deep breaths of fresh air, looks around for just a moment, reaches back into the small-screen TV, and calmly says, "Lynz, could I please borrow your camera again?"

The teen hands her dad the digital camera right through the screen of the second TV, which he took, and, from Taipei 101, pans around to make 10 seconds of video and two photographs, just for the sake of posterity.

#

Now, everyone is beginning to get squeamish about the crumbling of the cookie, seemingly into the most incredible order.

Yet, there are still things that need to be checked out.

Russell and Dianne head off out in the truck to try once again to pick up the now badly needed groceries, before the stores close.

#

"Groceries, kids!"

"Food!"

"Everything up to the kitchen, if you would."

"Except for that TV box. That's for the rec room again."

"It's your turn, Lyndsey; would you please set up the new TV for us?"

#

"TV's ready, Dad, Mom." Without exception, everyone is interested in this little operation.

Four pairs of eyes glue themselves to the second of the small-screen HDTVs that Russell Richardson has purchased while Dianne was shopping for the household and mealtime necessities.

"Go, James!"

"Good grief, another one!"

"It's hooked up to the *System* just like the other two sets."

"We're really onto something here, guys."

"This is unbelievable, Russell."

"Dianne," Russ asks, "would you please bring down the regular little TV from our bedroom?"

"Why?"

"Just so that we can keep an eye on NNN and see what's in the news, so that we can perhaps go see something live that's happening right now."

"It's almost ten o'clock; NNN might have a news report on for the start of the *Ethan Thomas 180°* show."

"Probably a couple of wars, a few murders, and lots of political intrigue, I guess."

Ethan Thomas, "We begin our program tonight with news of yet another apparent mining disaster in West Virginia.

"A report has reached NNN, which we are trying to confirm, that states that there has been an explosion in a coalmine.

"No word has yet been received about casualties, but it is feared that upwards of twenty miners may be trapped deep underground.

"The mine is located in the township of Paw Paw, West Virginia, about 10 miles south west of Morgantown, and the Interstate 79.

"Additional reports are expected in momentarily, and we will get these to you as soon as they become available to us.

"A reporter from our affiliate WKPP is en-route to the scene, and we'll get him to update us as soon as he is on-site.

"Meantime in other news …"

#

"Dad, let's 'drive' the *System* over to that mine, and see if there's anything we can do to help."

"OK, maybe Mom would like a crack at steering us up the I-79 to Morgantown and well play it by ear after that. It's dark there, too."

"I'd be willing to bet that it's darker where those miners are right now," the boy ventures.

Dianne, again, "Actually, there's something we can do about the darkness since we visited the Shoalhaven, if you remember."

She deftly handles the touch-pad remote so that the group is transported backward in time until it is once more in broad daylight. It becomes quite clear that the homemaker is quite adept at maneuvering the *System* with precision.

"It's a trip of almost 1,000 miles. Tricky bit will be finding Morgantown, and then Paw Paw. We've never driven in that area before."

"You'll have to get out your map and give me a hand."

" … Up the 275, until we hit the Interstate-75, then north till we hit the I-10. Take that to Jacksonville, then onto the I-26 …"

Well, Morgantown eventually shows up thanks to it being a junction of the I-79 and the I-68, two well-marked-out highways. Good old President Eisenhower!

Morgantown is only the start; now there is a need to do the ten miles in a southwesterly direction out of Morgantown.

Dianne is a driver's 'driver.' She first elevates the *System* so that it is possible to look down on the terrain as it flows underneath.

Then, in a very neat move on her part, she stops.

Moving forward in time until it is once again completely dark, and the family is back on real-time, it becomes a simple matter to pick out dozens of flashing red strobe lights and beacons, even at a range of several kilometers.

They are all on display; police cars, ambulances, hazmat trailers, fire trucks, and EMT vehicles, as well as mine company equipment. The night sky is well lit by the pulsing of flashing lights.

Dianne eases the *System* down to ground level.

From the pock-holed sofa, it is easy to keep an eye on both the *System* and the TV reports from New York.

NNN's Ethan Thomas continues to deliver the details of efforts required to rescue what now turns out to be a total of twenty-three miners.

"It has been reported by our correspondent in Paw Paw, West Virginia, that twenty miners are trapped in an unused tunnel that takes a dog-leg off to the left.

"This work area is well away from the main coalface, and it is hoped that efforts to reach them with food and water will continue throughout the night, and on until all the men are returned safely to the surface.

"The fate of the remaining three workers has not yet been determined and we are waiting for fresh word from the team of rescue workers that is now underground trying to reach the twenty trapped miners."

"Our coverage will continue live until we are able to give you some final results as to the fate of these men ..."

Lyndsey suggests, "Mom, when we did our tests with the *System* at the *Sunshine-Herald*, we were able to penetrate that huge solid sign without a single scratch."

"Are you saying what I think you're saying?" Dianne queries. "Do you mean you want me to 'drive' the *System* downward until it goes underground?"

James adds, "That may not be so hard, Mom. Look! Ethan Thomas is showing a map of the Paw Paw area and the exact location of the mineshafts.

"That info includes the tunnel these guys are supposed to be trapped in. So, we'll know which way to steer."

"Hold on, guys! What are we going to do with these miners even if we can find them? We can't take them in here."

"Why not?"

"What would we say to them, welcome to Florida?"

"That's not funny, Dad."

"We can't take them in because, if we do, the whole world will find out about the *System*, and we're really not ready for that news to get out yet."

"You mean that you could watch twenty, perhaps twenty-three men die just to preserve a secret?"

"Ouch ... Holy cow!" Russell cringes as he calls to mind the quandary faced by Prime Minister Winston Churchill of Great Britain during World War II.

Winston had to decide whether to alert the people of Coventry that, on that same night, their city was going to be bombed in November, 1940.

If he warns Coventry's citizenry of the impending raid, and they evacuate the area, the German Luftwaffe might figure out that the Brits had broken Hitler's secret codes.

"We could bring fresh air to the men and give them food and drink if they need it," Lyndsey adds.

"Yes, I suppose we could do that."

"If any of them are dead," James volunteers, "we could backpedal to a moment in time before they die, and get them into the house, through the *System*.

"It maybe that nobody knows that they have actually died. That way even if we did change history, so to speak, no-one would know anything about it."

No one gave an answer to this statement, since some were not sure what principle would apply in such an instance.

"OK, here goes," said Dianne, easing the *System* down below grade, following ET's maps, as James had suggested.

The view went totally black on all three sets. "Why have the lights gone out?" Dianne asks.

"It's alright, that's because we've gone underground. It's always this dark down here." Fortunately, the pun goes unnoticed.

The *System* moves smoothly and easily through the hard rock and coalfaces, until the boy asks, "Dad, where's your big million-candlepower flashlight?"

"In the truck, James, in the toolbox in the cargo area."

"Back in a minute."

#

"Got it!"

He puts his hand through the small-screen TV as far as he can, and shines the light, but it only helps when they come to a cavity in the rock where there is a space where the light can shine.

Suddenly, dim lights, but lights of any kind! "A tunnel; try going along it!"

With lights outside it is easier to navigate. Now they can try finding the tunnel where the explosion might have occurred.

It is helpful that they are able to cut corners by simply moving right through the bedrock walls of the tunnels. A few seconds of darkness at such times really are not that disconcerting.

It does take some time, but eventually they stumble over a place where the roof has collapsed, and rocks, timbers and coal would have blocked the path for a human rescue team.

Dianne continues to press ahead, simply 'intruding' the *System* into the fallen debris.

Back in darkness, James again shines the light through the small TV for everyone to be able to see Dianne's progress … "Great Scott! … Men! … Oh, no! Three men, but they're unconscious!"

In the mine it is still pitch black; the flashlight is very useful in being able to check out the injuries.

Lynz jumps to her feet and quickly climbs into the cavernous hole, while James continues to light her way with their dad's big flashlight.

"Dad, these men; they're dead! Not one of them has any vital signs.

"Mom, I'm coming back into the house.

"Can you back up in time until these men come back to life again?

"There has been no rock-fall just here, so they must have been killed either by shock or maybe a release of gas, perhaps methane. I have no way to know."

"Would it be OK" Dianne asks, "if I back up into the rock just to protect us from whatever it was, roll back in time until it happens and then come back into the tunnel about five minutes prior to the incident?"

"Deej, it's your call."

DJ ventures, "I'm not sure I like this! What do you think, Dad?"

Russell, "Perhaps Mom has the answer. But, as was mentioned before, no one knows these men have died yet, so perhaps no harm is done.

"But we need to think this over very carefully, in case there are situations in the future that require this same sort of decision.

"We don't want to stray away from following that base principle."

"Thanks, Dad."

"OK, Mom. Do what you suggested. Make sure we're in the rock deeply enough to prevent us from getting hit with whatever has caused this."

"OK, then," Dianne responds. "First I'll position the *System* just to the left of where the men are lying.

"Then I'll back off until we've penetrated the rock face and it closes in behind us, plus a couple of yards or thereabouts."

Dianne does as she has indicated and blackness again closes in on the scene.

"Could you turn James' timepiece this way so that I can read it? Is the old banger on Florida time, and with today's date?"

With the old timepiece in situ and properly adjusted, the young mother is able to back up in time for two and a half hours.

"That's about half an hour before the time NNN says the incident started.

"Now we can move back out of the rock face and, what do you see, Deej?"

David James, "LP, is this the three guys you saw that were dead in the tunnel?"

Lynz, "That's them, Mom; they're standing talking to each other now."

"OK, tell them that they are required in another section of the mine, immediately, and to get in here."

"Good morning, gentlemen. Management has asked us to pick you up and take you to another part of the mine, immediately. You can climb into this window, if you would, and we'll get you over there."

Good gracious! It actually works. The three miners clamber into the rec room through the *System*.

"Holy crow! What on earth happened to your loveseat?"

"It's a long story. Welcome to St. Pete's, men. We have to find the other location in the mine, so have a seat and perhaps Lyndsey can get you a drink."

"DJ, can you shine the light again, so that we can move on to the others."

As Dianne speaks, she is using the remote to re-adjust the actual time to match that shown on the clock on the wall, thus resetting the time to normal U.S. Eastern Standard.

The search for the other twenty men continues apace.

Dianne knows from the NNN reports that the 23 men had been located in two adjacent areas, so she works her way from where she had picked up the three resuscitated men.

Unknown to the group and its three guests, while Dianne is driving in circles, the incident occurred which has brought them the Paw Paw in the first place.

The sound and vibration of the explosion and subsequent rock falls goes unnoticed by them due to their own motion.

Driving in increasingly greater circles was taking a long time, until Russell says, "Is one of you gentlemen able to tell Mrs. Richardson where the other twenty men on your team are located?"

Before any one of the newly resurrected men can respond, Lyndsey calls out, "There they are, at the far end of that tunnel, lots of them!"

Mrs. Richardson eases up to the crowd of men and asks, "How many of you gentlemen are there?"

"Twenty-three altogether. Twenty of us here, and three others in a side tunnel."

Dianne, "OK, thanks. We already have the other three.

"We need you to climb into this elevator, so that we can get you off to the surface. So, if you men can step into this window, and come into our facility, we'll take you back to the surface."

"Two of our guys have broken arms, ma'am," the group leader advises.

Then, with a puzzled look on his face, "Who are you? How did you get in here?"

"We're a new underground rescue unit that … uh … specializes in helping miners that are trapped. We have a piece of equipment that functions well in this kind of environment."

Russell thinks, "Hey, 'keep 'em in the dark and feed 'em lots of fertilizer.' Boy, it works in the military, why not in a coalmine?"

The twenty climb into the *System*, injured ones first, and find themselves in the rec room of the Richardson's home.

They are clueless as to where they are or that they are now almost 1,000 miles away from Paw Paw, WV. and so trusting.

"Holee ... What happened to your sofa?"

DJ, "Drink anyone?"

Twenty-three strong, including two damaged,

Dianne 'flies' the *System* vertically, but, after the portal breaks the surface, Dianne creates some extra time for Lynz to do some temporary repairs on the damaged individuals.

She takes the *System* for a spin around the area of the mine.

At one point, she stops and moves in time so that it is broad daylight through the screen.

The miners are extremely impressed by this new piece of rescue equipment.

During the brief extra-curricular flight, the two injured men have their broken arms bandaged and put in a makeshift sling.

Lindsay creates the first-aid supplies from a bathroom towel. For splints, she uses long-handled kitchen spoons.

The girl is familiar with the nature of the injury thanks to an unusually intense first-aid course.

The training had been followed by several weeks of co-op work at a walk-in clinic in an industrial area of town. Broken arms are nothing compared to the action she had seen on that co-op.

Once Dianne comes into sight of the vehicles of the first responders, she again uses a time shift and returns the view to the darkness that prevails at the coalmine.

Despite their time traveling, Dianne has returned the whole group to real-time as shown by the antique corporate timepiece, matched to the rec room wall clock.

The emergency vehicles are still congregating at the mine head.

She works her way over to a poorly lit area, where the portal can disgorge its passengers in an obscure spot where no one is likely to be poking around.

Hence, their operation goes unobserved and the twenty-three miners can climb back through the *System* onto the soil of Paw Paw, West Virginia, their hometown.

Only the two bandaged individuals need any help, and that is only relatively minimal.

When the crowd of released captives walks around the corner of the building to the lighted area, where all the police, ambulance and fire vehicles are idling, with their beacons still lighting up the night sky, the screams of delight from their family members can easily be heard all the way to Florida.

#

"This is Ethan Thomas of *ET 180°*. As you know, tonight we devoted our entire show to coverage of that mining disaster.

"Personally, I was afraid that we were going to have some bad news for you, but we have just received an urgent call from our correspondent on the scene of that mine explosion earlier this evening.

"Folks, this has to be some kind of miracle! All twenty-three miners trapped below ground in that mine explosion are safe.

"They were returned to the surface by what the group has described as a 'newly-formed rescue team using specialized equipment and techniques.'

"Our reporter, along with other journalists at the site, has been told that 'the workers were taken into a large room … several noting that it contained a badly damaged daybed … and then, once back on the surface, they were asked to climb through a picture window to safety.'"

Ethan Thomas continues his report, advising that a mining company official had denied any knowledge of the new rescue unit or its specialized equipment.

"Sandra Hua, a spokesperson for the mine, reports that the company is looking forward with great interest to hearing from the men themselves, 'especially,' she notes 'about the nature of their speedy passage to the surface following a reportedly deadly explosion.'

"UMW officials have told *ET 180* that, 'Representatives of the United Mine Workers Union are hoping to clarify the situation once the miners have been taken to hospital for a routine check-up and debriefing.'

"Mrs. Hua has confirmed our earlier report that two miners each suffered a broken arm but the men are expected to be hospitalized only briefly for medical care for those injuries.

"The two will likely be released within a couple of hours as no additional problems have been reported. In fact, the two men who suffered a broken arm had apparently each been bandaged.

"The two arrived back on the surface, having already had the damaged limb splinted and put in a sling by the rescue unit's on-board personnel before reaching the surface.

"On behalf of all of us at *ET 180* and NNN, this is Ethan Thomas saying that we too look forward to hearing how this tragedy-in-the-making has been turned into a time of happy shouting and partying … and now, in other news …"

####

7 Aircraft Collide with Massachusetts Office Tower

NNN is again the bearer of news that will call the folks' attention to happenings in the world that require them to reach out to others.

The afternoon news program is the setting for a newsflash, "This item has just come into the NNN Newsroom from Boston this afternoon.

"We have word that what appeared to be two U.S. Navy F-16 aircraft have crashed into a high-rise office tower.

"Initial reports hint that the weather was misty, and that the two single-engined fighter jets may have simply gotten lost due to poor visibility and accidentally hit the building.

"There is no indication of terrorism here. The White House is already suggesting that this was a tragic error.

"We'll have an update on that story as soon as we can. Keep watching 'NNN Newsroom' for the latest on this terrible accident."

#

"Here is the latest on the Boston tragedy . . . The White House verifies that no terrorism is believed to have been involved in this crash of two F-16s into a building identified as the Massachusetts Tower in downtown Boston.

"Firefighters are on the scene and preliminary statements from on-site supervisors indicate that the two aircraft struck the Tower between about the twenty-forth and twenty-sixth floors.

"Several hundred people are employed at companies within the building.

"Phone calls and text messages from some of those who have escaped the flames state that all stairways above the twenty-second floor and up to the twenty-sixth are a mass of flames due to burning aviation fuel.

"This is preventing people from escaping from the higher floors.

"Our sources tell us that the Massachusetts Tower has thirty to thirty-five floors, meaning that the people working above the twenty-sixth floor who have survived the accident are unable to escape the holocaust.

"It has been reported to us that NTSB officials are en-route to the scene.

"The two pilots are feared to have died in the accident. We are awaiting word from the Pentagon as to their identities. Presumably, the information will not be released until … "

#

It is Thursday afternoon, a regular workday at the Richardson house; a regular school day for the kids at St. Pete's High School.

For the *System*, if the day is quiet, it will be spent silently staring at the *Sunshine-Herald* clock and calendar display.

First to spot the inferno as it appears on NNN on her kitchen TV was Dianne, who calls her husband, Russell, to look at the report.

Russ recalls the tragic horror of September 11, 2001; that almost magical date; the day the Twin Towers crumbled and fell.

He realizes that this is not likely to happen in the case of the Mass Tower since two F-16s would have neither the integral weight, nor the fuel load to create a repeat of that terrible occasion.

He remembers, too, that aerial ladders carried by fire trucks are only good up to the ninth floor.

"After that you're on your own," the fire chief had said, in a chilling statement he used at a conference Russell had attended some years before.

"Here in the NNN Newsroom, we are receiving fresh reports from Emergency Response authorities in the city of Boston.

"Scores of frantic mobile telephone calls are being received by 9-1-1 operators from individuals trapped above the twenty-sixth floor of the Mass Tower in Boston today.

"The emergency has arisen following an accident which saw two U.S. F-16 fighter-jet aircraft plough into the building.

"A spokesman for the City of Boston, which operates the Tower on behalf of the Commonwealth of Massachusetts, states that landline telephone communication with floors above the twenty-sixth, has been lost.

"NNN wishes to apologize for misinforming you earlier as to the identity of the two aircraft involved in this catastrophic accident.

"The Navy does not carry F-16s in its operational inventory. These were U.S. Air Force fighter-jets.

"Fire drills customarily advise employees inside taller buildings to head for the roof if the stairwells become inaccessible.

"However, in a panic situation like this, it is entirely possible that many will forget those instructions and crowd onto the lowest floor they can reach, to wait for the aerial ladders, which can't reach them anyway.

"Fire departments in cities with high-rise office towers lose dozens of people that way every year."

NNN News Staffer, "We are keeping a close eye on this story and will keep you abreast of any developments as they come in. Stay tuned to NNN Newsroom."

#

"Listen, Dianne, if we could do it for the miners, we can do it for these folks in Boston; what do you think?"

"Golly, Russ! That's four or five floors of offices, filled with workers! What will we do with all those people?

"Some of them could easily be injured, or even dead, and then what will we do?"

"Let's just play it by ear and take a few at a time. We'll just drop them off at ground level, as you did with the miners the other night. OK?"

Dianne says, "My mother told me there would be days like this!"

"Oh, come on, Di, you'll be great. If the kids come home in the middle of it, so much the better. This is fun!"

Russell is beginning to enjoy himself; he's starting to find his true strength. He has never learned how at a fast-food outlet's drive-through, but he obviously enjoys working under pressure.

He runs down the stairs to the carport door, opens the SUV, and picks up the GPS navigation equipment.

"I don't know why I didn't think of this before. We could have used this pesky thing the other night to get to the mine in Paw Paw, West Virginia.

"If you could get the Internet up on your mobile and get us a street address for the Massachusetts Tower, we can get there without having to make so many adjustments."

Having loaded the street address for the Mass high-rise, Russ places the GPS through the screen of the HDTV onto the rack James had fabricated from the wire coat hanger to hang his old watch on.

The former college student sits down at the controls of the 'Richardson shuttle' and sets the *System* to head off in a northerly direction, following the prompts of the GPS.

He chooses to travel at altitude, Dianne's trick, so they'll be able see the Cape Cod peninsula long before they reach Massachusetts airspace.

Long before he needs to think about finding Boston, the smoke from the Mass Tower can clearly be seen, so Russ ignores the routing instructions from the GPS and homes in on the fire's own marker beacon.

The *System* is working very smoothly and he selects a quiet, yet smoky area of the roof to settle down.

The low visibility of the 'exterior' side of the *System* is proving to be useful. The last thing the Richardsons need is a blind panic by hordes of frightened people, desperate to escape a funeral pyre.

"Stay here, Di! Take over the remote while I'm outside."

Stepping through the HDTV's large plasma screen feels good to him.

He crouches down in somewhat of an endeavor to maintain a low profile as he makes his way over to a group huddling together at the parapet of the roof.

"Quickly! Just the four of you; come this way. Now!"

The lone man and three women follow the tall frame as it walks back into the smoky area from which he had first emerged.

The group is completely unaware of the presence of the *System*, as its miniscule visibility is totally obscured by the thick smoke blowing around on the roof.

Ultimately, the small group is able to pick its way from the parapet at the edge of the roof over to where the backside of the screen is patiently waiting.

At Russell's urging, the small group climbs through the *System*, into the room where Dianne is sitting. Their rescuer is immediately behind them.

"Hi, folks! You all OK? We'll have you on the ground in a moment! Russell, are you alright to keep going?"

"OK, thanks, Di. It's just a bit hard to breathe out there."

Seconds later, and Dianne has done it again.

"There you go, ladies and gentleman. Sorry your trip to Florida was so short!"

The senior lady from the Mass Tower spoke on behalf of her group: "Thank you so very much; I'm sure we would have died if you hadn't gotten us down from there.

"The rescue helicopters were unable to get anywhere near us because of the smoke. Thank you again."

"Climb through the picture window here onto the ground in Boston, and you'll be just fine," Russell reassures.

"Who are you? How are you doing this? Are you from the government? What on earth happened to your sofa?" The rapid-fire questions come thick and fast.

Same reply as to the miners, with the necessary adjustments, of course: "We're a special, new, high-rise fire-rescue unit formed to handle situations exactly like this. This equipment is excellent for carrying out a rescue from skyscrapers in an emergency. Take care!"

She, along with her three companions, disappears into the disorganization and chaos of fire-fighting equipment, and masses of police and rescue vehicles outside the Massachusetts Tower.

"Di, that was great! You were incredible; so cool, calm and collected! . . . OK, back to the roof!"

"Heck! It would be so handy if we had another large-screen unit to work with, then we wouldn't need to shuttle back and forth between the roof and the ground.

"We could leave one unit positioned on top of the building and the other located at ground level and just pass the folks right through the rec room into the opposite *System*.

"Maybe we could even put the sets '*face-à-face*,' and then they wouldn't have to make comments about our lovely sofa."

Back to the roof it is. Next trip, Russ herds a larger group together that appears to be relatively calm. He ushers seven women and three men over to the *System*.

As the members of the group are helped through the exterior of the screen, "Hi folks, welcome to St. Petersburg. Is everyone OK?"

"Russ, are you still OK?"

"I'm fine, Dianne, just keep going."

"Hold tight, then, we're almost on the ground." The rescuees gape with open-mouths at the sight that can be seen on the three HDTV sets in the family's rec room.

"Who are you? How are you doing this? Are you from the government? What on earth happened to your sofa?" It was just like the first group. Questions just blast in one after the other.

Standard reply, "We're a special, new, high-rise fire-rescue unit formed to handle situations exactly like this. This equipment is excellent for carrying out a rescue from skyscrapers when the fire-truck ladders won't reach the high floors. Take care!"

With that, he directs them back to the large-screen TV and helps them to disembark.

"Thank you very much. What did you mean 'Welcome to St. Petersburg.

'This isn't Florida ...This is Massachuuussseettts' ... " was all that could be heard as, again, they are moved on by the Richardson's brand of shuttle diplomacy.

Dianne directs the *System* back to the smoky scene on the roof.

"Well, we're certainly meeting our share of Bostonians today, Di."

"Away you go, Hon. Be careful."

"Quickly! Just the ten of you; come this way, NOW!"

The stentorian tone reflects his growing anxiety at selecting larger groups of people for relaying through the *System*.

The miners had been twenty-three, but that had been an extreme case offering little alternative other than to take the entire crew.

Seven men and three women this time, in sheep-like fashion, followed the 'shepherd' across the roof.

Again, to the near-invisible shadow that represents the *System* on that smoke-blown roof.

It continues to be too dangerous for rescuers to use helicopters.

"Hold it! Why are you two in flight suits?" he demands of two of the men.

"Sorry, Staff," the first replies. "We punched out of our F-16s at the very last second. Our seats are zero-zero type and the parachutes deployed at about 600 feet and dropped us here on the roof."

"You mean you're the pilots of the planes that did this?" Russell asks. "Holy cow!"

"Sorry, Staff, we dove into an unusually heavy bank of low cloud, and there was just no way we could avoid hitting the building."

"Well, here's a piece of news for you. NNN has reported you as dead. You'd both better phone your wives."

"Into the window, folks," Russell instructs the whole group.

"One-at-a-time. That's it. We won't be in here for long."

Dianne is cheerful, as before. "Hi, folks! Welcome to 14 Dusty Miller Drive.

"You'll only be here for a few seconds, but in the meantime, is everyone OK?" she bubbles, glad to be of such enormous help.

"Russell, you OK to keep going, Hon?"

"I'm fine, thanks."

"Who are you people? ... How are you doing this?

"What part of the government are you from? ... What on earth happened to your sofa?"

Not again. Can no-one come up with an original question any more?

Reply number four, "We're a special, new, high-rise fire-rescue unit formed to handle situations exactly like this. This equipment is excellent for carrying out a rescue from high-rise office buildings. Take care!"

The eight civilians and two USAF pilots are ushered back into the 'window,' and sent on their way.

"Thank you very much for rescuing us. Have a nice day ... Hey, just a minute, ma'am. The city of Boston doesn't have a Dusty Miller Drive. Where are weeeee ... ?" The voice fades into the incredible cacophony of sound outside the Massachusetts Tower.

#

Five more trips are made, identical to that one, and the crowd on the roof quickly dissipates.

"That's it, Dianne," Russell proclaims.

"Now someone with the means to do so will have to let any employees congregating on the floors above the flames know that they should move onto the roof, where they can be cared for."

#

Local officials obviously have no knowledge of how the folks from the roof are managing to get down to ground level.

#

NNN Staff, "Back at the Newsroom ... a quirk to this unfolding story is puzzling authorities in Boston.

"Well over sixty people trapped on the roof of the flaming Mass Tower in Boston have mysteriously been transported from the top of the high-rise office building down to the ground.

"Local and State police and FBI, as well as U.S. Air Force investigators are trying to track down the precise nature of this enigmatic but timely rescue.

"The building was the site of a tragic accident this afternoon, when two F-16 fighter jets crashed ...

#

"Keep tuned to NNN Newsroom for the very latest update, which will come to you as soon as it comes in to us."

#

Again, from an NNN News staffer, "A further report has come in from Boston in connection with the tragedy at the Mass Tower this afternoon.

"Rescue officials have stated that people trapped on lower floors just above the flames, have been warned to move to the roof, where it has been cleared for the helicopters to land.

"Hopefully this will see an end to the threat to their well-being.

"A few people are reported killed in the crash of the two F-16s into the high-rise, and many are injured.

"Our reporter is on the scene now and we're going to get him on camera now to bring you the latest now that we have been able to re-establish contact with him and can show you video of the carnage in Boston."

#

"An incredible announcement was made a short while ago by the Boston Fire Department.

"Officials state that sixty people were miraculously brought down from the roof to ground level during the conflagration.

"Of that number, two of those individuals have identified themselves as the U.S. Air Force pilots, whose planes tragically crashed into the tower, causing the holocaust.

"Both are reported to be in fine shape and have been handed over to military authorities for debriefing.

"Stay tuned to NNN Newsroom for the very latest updates, which will come to you as soon as they come in to us."

#

"Di, we have to do what you mentioned before!"

"What did I say?"

"You know, about buying another large-screen TV so that we can transfer people directly from one TV to the other. That way we don't have to worry about them coming into our home in droves."

"If we're going to be involved in large-scale operations like the Mass Tower, then that will definitely be a good investment."

"I'll see to it tomorrow," Russell asserts.

#

"Mom, Dad! Have you been using the *System*?"

"Oh, we just took a 1,200 mile trip up around Cape Cod; nothing spectacular."

####

8 Opportunity Knocks But Once

James was nearest the front door when the bell rang.

"Mr. Thomas! … Dad, come quick! … It's Ethan Thomas from NNN!"

"You must be Russell."

"Where did you get my name?"

"Actually, it wasn't as difficult as you might think.

"People were telling us a week or ten days ago that they had been rescued from a fire on top of the Massachusetts Tower in Boston after two F-16s hit the building the week before last.

"Some told us there was a Florida connection; others that it was a place in St. Petersburg, one group even insisted it was Dusty Miller Drive.

"You're the only Richardson on Dusty Miller Drive in St. Pete's, Florida, so here I am."

"Where did you get my family name?"

"One of the miners in Paw Paw, WV, said you asked that 'Mrs. Richardson' be given directions to the other miners trapped down that mine shaft.

"Two plus two equals Russell Richardson at 14 Dusty Miller Drive, n'est ce-pas?" he said, flexing his high school French.

"I guess you'd better come in." Russell ushers the honored guest down to the rec room.

"You have a lovely home here, folks … Good grief! What on earth happened to your sofa?

"It looks as if somebody took a machine-gun to it! I hope they only hit the sofa, and not someone from your family!"

"I guess you're here about the *System*?"

"I beg your pardon! The *what*?"

"We have been calling it the *System*, because no other name we come up with seems to fit what it does."

"Coffee?" Lyndsey inquires.

"Yes, please; black, no sugar; thanks."

"Dad?"

"Yes, please, Lynz."

"Is this the stuff you have been telling people is some sort of equipment that is specially designed for carrying out rescues from mines and skyscrapers?"

"That's right! I told them that my wife and I were part of a special, new, high-rise fire-rescue unit formed to handle situations exactly like theirs. I told the miners that we were a special new mine-rescue unit."

"Do you mean they actually swallowed that? Wow!"

As Dianne was the only one in the upper areas of the house, she was elected to get the front door the second time the bell rang that day.

"Di, that'll be my Mom and Dad," Russell calls up the stairs. "Could you let them in please?"

"It would be very helpful if you could give me a rough idea of what this is all about, so that I can formulate some strategy as to how we can go about handling the situation."

"My son, James, was the one who stumbled over this ... DJ, would you please tell Mr. Thomas what happened to you a couple of weeks ago?"

"Ethan, please."

"Ethan, excuse me, please. Dad, Mom, this is Ethan Thomas of NNN.

"Ethan, may I introduce my dad, Buckminster Richardson, and my mom, Ladybird. They have been in on this phenomenon just about right from the start.

"If you'd like to take a seat, we'll get DJ to tell you how all this got under way, including how the sofa got itself all shot up."

James begins, "This sofa was where it all started. I was sitting right here on February 21, watching TV, and surfing the channels to find something to watch.

"Don't ask me how or why," the boy says, "but, without any warning, a World War II U.S. marine suddenly stuck his rifle out of the TV, and started blasting away at me. It was the marine who did the damage to the seat."

"You're kidding, of course," the news anchor reasoned.

"That's what I said when Dianne and I got home from a trip, and saw this mess."

Once more a clarion call from the doorbell upstairs.

"Good grief! Who could that be?" Russell moans.

"I'll get it," Buck volunteers. The late-model baby boomer walks up the stairs to the main entrance.

Ladybird watches as her husband climbs, admiring his still-agile step, realizing that he has not lost his military bearing.

Russell asks, "Wait till my dad gets back. He's been in on this almost from the start, and I always appreciate his input."

From upstairs, "Chuck! Jackie! It's months since we saw you last! How are you guys? It's good to see you. Come on in, everybody!

"The family's down in the rec room. Something unbelievable has happened! You'll never guess who's downstairs visiting with them."

"Holy cow, guys. Who's not here?" Charles Grover, better known to all as Chuck, or Pop, is the first one down. "Dianne, what on earth is going on here? It's almost two weeks since we heard from you last."

Jackie, better known as Jay or J.G., follows Chuck down the stairs and takes her turn at rollicking her daughter, Dianne.

"What are you all doing jammed up at one end of the sofa? Good grief! What on earth happened to your chesterfield?

"Ladybird. How are you? It's so good to see you!

"Ethan Thomas, NNN! ... What are you doing here? ...

"What's going on? ... Russell?"

The NNN anchor is already on his feet and approaches with his usual friendly manner.

Dianne does the honors, "Ethan, these folks already know who you are, so I'd better introduce my father, Chuck Grover, and my mother, Jackie."

"Dad, Mom, I'm sorry we didn't get in touch with you lately. We're all OK, just so that you don't get alarmed, but something incredible has happened! Ethan is here to check it out."

Dianne went on to enlarge briefly, "Something weird has happened to our new HDTV. We don't have any clue as to why, but it's turned into some sort of time machine.

"As a result of that, we're able to travel anywhere in the world, even climb in and out of the house, right through the set.

"What is even more incredible is that the TV also has the capability of being able to travel through time.

"Ethan stumbled over a couple of things we had done, while we were using the TV to help some people through some difficulties.

"He was able to track us down, and is here to get further information for a program he is planning to do.

"DJ was just about to explain to Ethan exactly how the whole thing got started, and what caused the daybed to get blasted, because that's how it all happened.

"DJ, can you start over with your explanation so that Granddad and Nanny can get in on the bottom rung of the ladder."

James, just once more, "This sofa is where it all started. I was sitting right here on February 21, surfing the TV channels to find something to watch.

"There was no warning at all, and then a World War II U.S. marine suddenly stuck his rifle out of the HDTV, and started blasting away at me. It was the marine who actually did the damage to the seat."

"DJ, could you let Ethan see what you showed us to prove what had happened to the television?"

James picks up the remote control touch-pad and adjusts the date display so that the old analog display at the edifice shows February 21, 1945, then directs to *System* to go from the newspaper office in St. Pete's to Iwo Jima.

After a trip lasting some ninety seconds, he shows Ethan Thomas and his own maternal grandparents the massive buildup of ships offshore of Iwo Jima.

The youngster time-shifts to 5:00 p.m., and shows everyone, in live action, USS *Saratoga* being targeted by Japanese *kamikaze* aircraft.

He backs up and shows the same action again and again. Then transfers the *System* to the other side of the fleet and shows the same scene from another angle.

Lyndsey does her best to glide down the stairs with a tray of coffee cups, custom-made for each drinker, and skillfully hands them out to the customers of the Richardson restaurant.

Ethan Thomas is puzzled. "I just have to say that this cannot be! TVs just don't act like that all by themselves!"

"I must agree with that, Russell," Chuck Grover opines. "TVs can only show what the TV station puts out; they can't just run off and show whatever they like."

James returns to the *System*'s original location and keeps the HDTV displaying the action off the Pacific island's coast.

"I'm sorry, Ethan!" Russell continues to explain. "That's the way it is.

"Look! We kept a pouch of notes we picked up on an island called Ie Shima. It's just about a half-mile northwest of Okinawa which was the site of a huge military campaign during April of 1945."

"What do you mean when you say you 'picked up' a pouch of notes?" ET asks.

"Put your hand on the screen of the TV," Russell challenges.

Ethan reaches out and, balancing his coffee in one hand, places his other hand where the solid surface of a TV screen would normally be, but his hand finds nothing! He is able to put his hand right into the TV without harm.

"Heavens!" he exclaims.

Chuck Grover frowns in puzzlement; he rises from his seat, and walks over to the TV and does the same thing as ET did before him.

He too reaches out with his hand to touch the screen of the TV, and similarly finds nothing to stop his hand from penetrating the seemingly lighted surface.

“That’s right, Ethan, Chuck. If we were over dry land, instead of the Pacific Ocean, you would be able to step right through that HDTV, even into the year 1945.

“That is exactly what Buck, my dad, did, on that same day DJ spoke about, a couple of weeks ago, and came up with a souvenir of the fighting on Okinawa, as well as the leather case.”

“Souvenir?”

“Yes. I went for a quick walk during the time the fighting was taking place and found a .45-caliber automatic that one of the soldiers had dropped,” Buckminster clarifies.

ET, “What did you say was in the pouch?”

“Well, here is the briefcase, right here,” says Russell, walking over to the unlighted fireplace, retrieving and opening the leather *objet d’art.*

“Inside is a portfolio of papers each bearing a signature … take a look at how these documents are signed and dated.

“We’ve put a page protector on each sheet to keep it from getting damaged … this is original stuff we’re convinced is genuine Ernie Pyle.

“We recovered it off that island beside Okinawa, within a few hours of his death on April 18th, 1945.

“Some soldiers threw it away. We saw them do it. I guess they couldn’t see a use for it with him having been killed.

“Someone here suggested donating the whole collection to the Ernie Pyle Museum in Dana, Indiana, to let the folks at the museum verify that it really is his work.”

ET again, “Hey, not a bad idea! Good thinking!

“My goodness, this is serious stuff. Pyle is an icon to people in my industry. I really thought, at first, that you guys were joking.

“Russell, could you do me a favor?” ET asks. “Would you mind taking me over to dry land, so that I can try the climb-through onto the island?”

“Sure. Lyndsey can do that for you. Lynz, could you ‘drive’ Ethan over to Iwo and let him try out a little extra vehicular activity.

“Maybe, first, move ahead to September or October, so that the war is over and there’s no more shooting going on.

“Ethan, you might watch how Lyndsey does this; it’s extremely quick and hyper accurate.”

Lynz reaches into the screen and recovers the corporate timepiece, but she finds it is unnecessary to make any adjustments to reflect an April, 1945, date.

Replacing the chronometer on James' wire rack, she time-shifts forward to September 3, 1945, one day after the Pacific phase of World War II ended.

After 'driving' over to the local beach, "There you go, sir," Lyndsey announces.

"Ethan, are you OK with this alone, or would you prefer a chaperone?" Russell invites.

"Could one of you give me a demonstration first?" he asks.

"Dianne, would you do the honors?" Russ asks apprehensively, since Dianne has never been through the screen.

"I guess so, otherwise you'll never let me rest," she responds.

Walking over to the TV, she puts her left leg in, ducks to clear her head and then draws her right leg through the device.

Those movements put her on the black-sand beach on the eastern shore of Iwo Jima.

She looks around to see if there is any sign of life around and finds nothing at all. Far off in the distance she can see Suribachi's volcano-like shape.

Just seven months earlier, anyone standing on this beach would have attracted sniper, machine-gun, artillery, and even tank fire, which would have assured a quick death.

At this time of year though, there is no risk. It is totally quiet, a very peaceful haven, although it certainly still bears the marks of the heavy fighting of the previous February and March.

"When you're ready, Ethan," she calls back into the house.

The news anchor steps over to the HDTV and copies Dianne's moves; left foot first, ducking down to avoid damaging his superstructure; then the right leg.

Now Ethan Thomas joins Dianne on Iwo Jima in 1945, all without firing a shot!

"I really did. I thought you guys were joking," ET admits.

Next move comes from Chuck Grover. The maternal granddad to the two teens is completely spellbound by the *System* and simply cannot resist trying it out with a little more than his hand.

He steps over to the set, and firmly plants his feet onto the black beach of Iwo Jima, seventy years ago.

He strides over to where Ethan and Dianne stand facing the exterior surface of the portal, both still in amazement at the phenomenon they are experiencing.

The folks in the house are able to follow the conversation without difficulty as Ethan continues speaking.

"You know, if I managed to find you, many others could do the same, including the FBI, the CIA, the paparazzi, even the mob. You're going to be swamped here any day now."

The NNN news specialist responds slowly to the growing mental realization of the situation and addresses the youngsters' dad through the screen.

"Russell, since I was the one who found you, would you be agreeable to letting me have an exclusive interview with you for *Ethan Thomas 180°* on my network?"

"Ethan, you've been so empathetic and understanding, that I'm inclined to agree that this would be quite acceptable. What do you think, James, Lyndsey; this is pretty much your action?"

"Wow! What's to say no to?" James excitedly agrees.

Arriving back at the rec room level, Lyndsey is just as positive.

Dianne, on Iwo Jima with Ethan concurs, "I agree with the children. This really should belong to humanity, not just to us. We don't have the resources to exploit its capabilities anyway."

"True, Babe! That's a good point," Russell affirms.

"Can Lyndsey follow us if we walk along the beach, so that we can continue talking?"

"Give her a try," Dianne said.

Dianne, along with her father, and the family's honored guest do an about-face and turn south.

The trio walks in step along the beach in the direction of Suribachi, and Lynz follows; close behind at first, then carefully she circles around her mother, grandfather, and Ethan

The young girl rotates the *System* one hundred and eighty degrees, and successfully positions the set, so that those in the house are leading the way for the beachcombers.

This way the conversation can continue without shouting.

#

Next, it's the turn of the carport doorbell to ring.

"Would one of you kids get the door?" Russell asks. Since Lyndsey is 'driving,' James disappears down the stairs.

"Dad, it's a shipment of a few boxes. Two are small and the other is a big box. They're from the Electronics Superstore!" James calls upstairs to his dad.

"That's fine, Deej. I've been waiting for that delivery. It's a TV! Just sign for it and ask the driver to put it inside the carport door."

#

ET, "What would you think if I simply identified you as a family that has discovered a means of transporting people and things not only around the earth, but also into the past?"

"No objections to that."

"As a matter of interest, how far back have you gone in history?" ET asks.

"Well, the kids were a bit bored one day and decided they wanted to be helpful to someone, so they keyed in the year '1492' and took a trip over to London, England.

"They checked in at the Tower of London with a guard named John Summerfield as to what the actual date was, as folks back in those days weren't quite as sensitive as we are about the passage of time," Russell says.

The Grovers are fascinated by the continuing banter between the correspondent and the host family.

ET, "I know I'm going to wind up with egg on my face here, but what exactly made them settle on 1492?"

"I don't know if you'll believe this, but they thought they'd like to look up Christopher Columbus on his 'voyage of discovery,' and see if he needed any help.

"It turned out that he was glad to see them, because he was sailing north instead of west. They set him straight and told him to follow some shore birds which would lead him toward land."

"What a relief! The Americas almost went undiscovered. Maybe if he had continued north he would have discovered Nova Scotia or

Newfoundland. How that would have changed history is anybody's guess!

"What have you done about traveling into the future?"

"Not a thing! I think we were simply too busy examining historical things, and solving problems in mines and high-rise office towers, rather than peering into what hasn't actually happened yet.

"To be truthful, we're studiously dodging around that issue, because we want to avoid making changes to either history or the future, where there might be a long term consequence.

"On top of that, we're trying to live our normal lives."

"What would you think if we just identify the means of teleportation through time as being a television set and leave it at that?

"We could just say that you had come up with a way to maneuver the time and place and the set would carry out your requests.

"There shouldn't be a need to mention anything about the touch-pad remote control or the part it plays in the operation.

"That way, we might be able to protect your secret for a while, at least until you can get a handle on it.

"Perhaps we could say that the *System* is the subject of a patent application.

"OK, I'm coming back into the house," the correspondent says. He steps back into the rec room, and says, "I don't know what to think … that's more than fascinating."

Chuck has a private question to ask Dianne. "Sweetheart, why didn't you let your mom and me know about the *System*?

"You've known about this for weeks, yet you never said a word."

"Dad, I'm sorry, but we had no idea what it was that we had stumbled over."

"How did Buck and Bird get involved?"

"Pop, that wasn't our doing ... Buck found out about it before Russell and I did.

"We weren't even home. He dropped by to say hello just after the marine had shot off his rifle into the sofa.

"Once Buck got wind of what was going on, he called Ladybird to come over right away.

"Honestly, we're still trying to get our heads around this ourselves.

"You know, Dad, we would have called you in the next day or two, anyway. We're going to need you both to help us in the future.

"There's far too much work for even six people to do using the *System*.

"We can pick you up at the house and you can come over and join us first thing tomorrow morning. Why don't you join us for breakfast; we'll pick you up at 8:00 a.m."

"OK, I'll let your mom know what you said, and we'll be ready for you to pick us up tomorrow in the SUV."

"No, Dad. Not in the SUV. We'll pick you up with the *System*; it's much more energy-efficient."

Meanwhile, back in the house, continuing his earlier thought, Ethan expresses another idea. "You know, we could even do the interview with you 'off-camera.'

"That way we keep you incognito. It might help to keep the wolves at bay for a while. What do you think?"

Russell, "That might be the best way to go about it."

"OK, let me get my producer updated on this, and I'll let you have some idea as to how he feels we can best handle this."

"While you do that, Ethan, we're going to set up the new large-screen TV," Russell states.

"Gramps, could you and Grandma give us a hand to set up the new TV," DJ asks Buck.

"Sure! Whereabouts do you want it positioned?" Buckminster asks.

"Dad told me this new set is equipped with a base on castors, so if you can rig it up and roll it in ready to use beside the other HDTV, that would be great."

Buck, "If you kids could give us a hand up with the boxes from the carport, that would be very helpful."

"OK, right away!"

In no time, the boxes are in the family room and the contents are stripped of all outer wrappings, which are dutifully returned to the lower level of the house.

The base unit upon which the new HDTV is to sit is quickly assembled and equipped with its casters.

Buck decides to test the base by putting his left foot on top of it and propelling himself across the rec room, using it as a skateboard. His opinion is, "This works just fine! It's really smooth-running."

The flat-screen TV is relatively simple to put into operation. It only requires a plug to be inserted into a nearby outlet.

A connection to the *System* is obtained by merely rolling the new acquisition to a location beside its older brother, and, *voila*! Iwo Jima hove into sight.

This is overwhelming for everyone, including Ethan Thomas, who, although still deep in conversation on his mobile with his producer in New York, is watching every move.

Ladybuck is the one who breaks the ice. She steps over to the new TV, holds her skirt down and enters, right leg first, into the 'dream zone' of Iwo.

She walks by way of the black sand over to the backside of the older, original portal and manages her most ladylike step back into the rec room.

Her first EVA has been successfully accomplished without incident. This proves that the second, new, large-screen HDTV is definitely hooked up to the family's amazing discovery.

The family now has four units hooked up to the *System*: Two 70" flat-screens, and two small-screen TVs that are used for testing and experimentation.

The fifteen-inch units can additionally be used for the teleportation of smaller items of equipment, such as digital cameras, mobile phones, GPS equipment, documents, etc.

Ernie Pyle's portfolio would easily fit diagonally through the screen should there arise a necessity.

#

Without having to have it surgically removed from his ear, Ethan disconnects himself from his mobile telephone and apologizes for his long conversation with his producer.

He, Ethan says, is so fascinated with what ET has told him, that he has decided he needs to see it for himself.

"May I invite him to come down here first thing tomorrow? He would arrive at the airport at about 8:30."

"Whatever you think is appropriate, Ethan," Russell acknowledges.

"Thinking about it, Ethan, why don't you and your producer come for breakfast at 8:00 a.m., and we'll all be able to enjoy a meal together before we get started."

"I have to look after preparing for *ET 180º* tonight. Could you take me back to New York with the *System*?"

"Awesome! I'll be at NNN in time to catch my producer, and I can set him up for the morning."

"OK. I'll get my mother to take you to New York now, and, if it's OK with you, perhaps the two of you, you and your colleague, would join us for breakfast tomorrow.

"We'll pick both of you up in New York at about 7:55 a.m. so as to have you here for eight o'clock, if that's OK with you."

"Alright by me! I'll make sure he's ready for pick-up, too."

"Mom," Russell queries Ladybird, "could you 'shuttle' Ethan to New York and drop him at the NNN building."

"Only in exchange for breakfast for Buckminster and me tomorrow," she jokes.

"Done deal!" Russell replies. "We'll be glad to have you."

"Would you like me to leave the *System* parked on NNN's roof overnight? That way we can pick the two of you up in the morning. No traveling!"

Handshakes and expressions of thanks all around, and Ladybuck 'steers' her way to the NNN headquarters, with a navigational assist from Ethan, and 'lowers' the *System* gently onto the roof to let ET disembark.

She 'parks' the *System* about twenty feet above the roof, well away from the helicopter pad.

####

9 General George Washington in 1776

Ethan Thomas and his producer, Ron Pfeffer, and a third man, a stranger, climb aboard.

Both Ron and the other newcomer embark with much hesitation, although ET has briefed them extensively about the capabilities of the *System*.

All three receive the usual warm welcome from the family.

Ethan makes the necessary introduction for the unknown man who has arrived with him and his producer.

"Folks, I'd like you to meet a personal friend of mine; this is Alexander Allca, but you can call him Alex."

The correspondent introduces him individually to each of the eight of the members of the family group.

After all eleven present enjoy a warming breakfast together, enjoying each other's company, Ethan continues with his introduction of Alex Allca.

"Alex is a rather interesting personality, although you may not be familiar with his name.

"He's the founder and chief executive officer of the Alexander Allca Foundation.

"There was a reason why I invited him to meet you all this morning.

"I spent quite a while talking with Alex last night, explaining the portal that has turned up in your home and, to say the least, he was absolutely spellbound.

"You had related to me yesterday that you would like to find some way to franchise this technology, but you do not have the financial backing to be able to set up such an arrangement.

"Well, Alex expressed an interest in seeing the *System* for himself.

"Frankly, he could easily be in a position to offer some ideas as to how you might go about marketing this through a non profit organization, just like his own foundation.

"So, show the three of us exactly what it is you have got here, and then we'll let him make up his mind what suggestions he wants to make."

Russell stands up to speak briefly, "Well, DJ is the one we have voted into taking the lead at the moment.

"Actually, the phenomenon turned up while he was watching the TV, so the family is happy to let him represent us.

"James."

"Thanks for coming, everyone," James greets, becoming the host for the morning.

"We appreciate you joining us for this session this morning.

"From our own personal experience so far, we know you will not be disappointed.

"For our demonstration outing we are heading off up north to a little spot called McConkey's Ferry Inn, in Pennsylvania.

"We're going to make this a low-tech trip to show you how we had to go about our time travels in our early days using the *System*.

"Lynz, would you 'drive' for us?"

"Grandma Ladybuck, could you be the GPS navigator? I've written the address for a location in Penn State on this piece of paper.

"You'll have to go to this place first, and then Lyndsey will need to travel backward in time for 7.5 seconds.

"That will put you outside a newspaper office back in the seventeen hundreds.

"Then one of us can check the date on a copy of the paper's front page that they will put in the window each morning.

"Once we're sure we have the correct date, we'll be able to go on to our final destination."

"Where are we off to, DJ?" Ethan asks.

"See if you can figure that out when we get to our first checkpoint," the teen challenges. "I'll supply the date and the personalities. See if you can figure out the event."

"The first stop is the *Philadelphia Mercury*, one of the oldest American newspapers, dating back to the late seventeenth century.

"Our interest today lies in activities that took place on December 25, 1776, reported the following day, and concern the activities of a certain American general."

"By the way, it's a good idea to avoid saying 'Christmas,' because back in the 1770s many American colonists shunned the celebration, considering it to be an 'English' custom.

"'A Christmas Carol' by Charles Dickens is considered by many to be the catalyst that brought the once 'pagan' holiday into favor with Americans.

Lyndsey pulls up outside the Philly journal's offices and, while DJ calls the numbers aloud, using his own wristwatch as a timer, she backs up in time for just over seven seconds.

She pauses at his command and no one could miss the fact that the building housing the newspaper has drastically changed its configuration.

Before their eyes, the towering skyscraper melts down to a small storefront with a modest sign proclaiming the paper's name.

Buckminster volunteers to head out to check the date on the newspaper in the window. James agrees and, as soon as pedestrian traffic quiets down, Buck carries out the extra vehicular activity.

"February 18, 1777," the teenagers' paternal grandfather calls out.

He returns to the *System* and takes his seat once more.

"That thing in the window is the front and back of a four-page newspaper. I thought there would be more of it."

"Lyndsey, could you move us backward again. This time it will be just about eight weeks?"

"Deej, could you please straighten the old watch on the rack for me? It's much easier than counting days and nights."

With the adjustment duly made; the chronometer in place, Lyndsey slowly 'cruises' into the past, and the group watches with fascination as the days repeatedly turn into nights.

"We used to have to count the light and dark periods to calculate how far we had gone backward.

"OK, hold it there, Lynz!"

"Grandpa Buck, could you do the honors?" the teen asks.

After the customary check to make sure the coast is clear, the call comes back, "December 27, 1776."

Again, Buckminster returns to the house.

"Thanks, Gramps. That agrees precisely with the watch."

"OK, Lynz. We need to go two more days to about noon on December 24 of that same year."

Lyndsey backpedals until the watch indicates is the right date and time. Then, with DJ's agreement, she stops.

Ethan calls out to James, "Deej, before you move on, can I try something out on the street in Philly?"

"Sure, go ahead," the master of ceremonies replies.

"Can I come with you," Alex Allca asks. "This is my hometown, after all."

"Be my guest," the news anchor responds.

ET is already on his feet and steps into the rustic urban scene. Lynz pans the *System* so that all can see what he is doing.

Allca joins him and together they coolly walk into the newspaper's office, and Thomas introduces himself.

"Good day, sir, my name is Ethan Thomas. I'm with a newsgathering organization called the National News Network in the city of New York.

"My friend is Alexander Allca. Mr. Allca is an investment counselor here in Pennsylvania. We just arrived back in town."

He asks the publisher the date and local time, to which the early-American executive replies, "December 24, 1776, and the hour is 10:30 o'clock."

At those latter words, James chuckles to himself as he sees the corporate watch is displaying exactly that time.

Despite the fact that this will come close to giving the newspaperman an apoplectic fit, the NNN anchor shows the man his twelve-megapixel digital camera.

He explains that this is a device that helps him to draw portraits.

He asks permission of the publisher to permit the small, shiny box to draw his picture, to which the man agrees.

Getting him to smile is not too difficult, and switching the camera to its video mode, he takes about five seconds of footage.

He releases the shutter button and reverses the camera, displaying to his subject the footage he has just taken. The man's jaw hangs down, as, for just this one time in his life, he sees himself in anything other than a mirror, a window, or a lake.

"Thank you, sir. May I inquire as to your name?"

"Benjamin Fraser."

"My grateful thanks to you, Mr. Fraser," he says.

Before Ben can ask him how to arrange the purchase of such a magic box, Ethan ushers Alex quickly to the door and back to the *System*.

Thanks to a perceptive 'chauffeur,' the portal is patiently waiting back outside the office.

First verifying the lack of eyewitnesses to their movements, the two men return to the rec room.

"Wow, wasn't the look on his face something precious?" he laughs.

"OK, is everyone ready for the final leg of our trip?" DJ questions, but it is rhetorical.

"Where to now, Deej?" Lyndsey asks. "You said you wanted me to zero in on another location."

"That's OK! What you can do now is take us northeast for a distance of just about 25 miles.

"When we figure you're close to our destination, you can slow down, and we'll all keep an eye out for a river that's about two hundred and fifty yards wide.

"We'll use the waterway as a landmark to find the spot we're after." James has spent the night researching this information, so he is confident of the success of this project.

After Lynz has been 'cruising' fairly slowly for a short while, and everyone else is beginning to get the impression that the twenty-five miles are about up, the first call comes from Lynz's maternal grandmother, Jackie Grover.

"Is that the river you're looking for, James? … Look, off in the distance, behind those trees, about one quarter of the way across the screen from the left side."

"That has to be it, JG! Thanks, that's good spotting," James commends.

"What we're looking for is a small town on the far side of the watercourse. It's actually in the state of New Jersey. Today, it's a city called Trenton, but, in 1776, it's a part of small-town America.

"Now, we have to follow the river to the north for about ten miles.

"It doesn't have bridges for us to count to guide us as to how far. So we have to guess again as to how far ten miles is."

Once more, Lyndsey wheels around to the new vector, and follows the river below, at a height of only around thirty feet.

Onshore, the precipitation can be observed quickly forming drifts.

On the water, however, ice crystals are rapidly becoming solid ice, thick enough to cause problems for the American general the group is traveling all this way to see.

The present time outside is just shortly after that given by the publisher of The *Philadelphia Mercury*, namely, 10:35 a.m. The date has not changed and remains at December 24, 1776.

So, they are some forty hours short of the event to which James has invited everyone.

Lyndsey continues to conduct the group in a northerly direction, still dutifully following the course of the waterway.

"DJ, are we there yet," the girl asks. This sounds very familiar to most of the adults present, but they collectively keep their thoughts to themselves and let the opportunity go by.

"About one more mile, and you'll come into sight of our objective, Lynz," her brother replies.

One half-minute later, with the river still in the center of the view, DJ calls attention to a multitude of men encamped on the west bank of the Delaware River.

His sibling slows to a crawl, then stops and rotates to have the crowd in the middle of the screen.

"Who are these men, James?" his grandfather Buckminster queries.

"You'll have to guess, Gramps. Think about it, though.

"You're at the Delaware River, just north of Trenton, New Jersey, in the year 1776. What part of this information might give you a clue?"

"I can see this is your idea of an American history morning.

"Great question, DJ!" Alex says.

He adds, "This is an awesome event in our country's history.

"These troops are with the Continental Army, just before it is led across the Delaware River, back on the morning of December 26, 1776.

"The general is none other than George Washington, who will later become America's first president."

"James, will we be able to watch the actual event? This is exciting?" says his mother, Dianne.

"We all know the outcome, but it's fascinating to think that we'll be watching the occasion live."

"For sure, Mom! We'll watch the crossing in a little while, but first we have to get Lynz to do a bit more time shifting first."

As Dianne answers James, and while the boy responds to his mother, Lyndsey propels the *System* forward slowly in time.

At the same time, she also changes direction so as to rotate in ever-increasing circles, so that each tour of the area encompasses a larger circle than the preceding turn.

This gives them the opportunity to oversee the entire site of the crossing, as well as the encampment of the small expedition from the Continental Army.

She concentrates on the encampment, looking out for the general in his gilt-edged uniform. The group has to watch for a person who looks somewhat younger than the George Washington on the present $1.00 bill.

As time progresses, she 'drives' to lower and lower altitudes, so that, unseen by the soldiers below them, they are able to scan for the heroic figure, without needing to break out Russell's binoculars.

One tent, which appears to receive visits from junior officers on numerous occasions, is given extra attention by the group.

It takes an ex-military person in the rec room to say, "That guy's a colonel, you can see his insignia. Next step up the promotion ladder for him is 'general.'"

"See if you can get close enough so that we can have a word with him," Ethan Thomas asks.

Lynz quickly drops the screen down to ground level, moves over toward the officer in question, and brings the *System* to a halt. ET is the self-appointed interrogator of this officer.

He eases himself out of the screen for his extra-vehicular activity and approaches the colonel.

"Good morning, colonel!" he begins. "My name is Ethan Thomas, and I'm a news correspondent, most recently at the *Mercury* in Philadelphia.

"What information are you able to share with our readers about your upcoming crossing of the Delaware River over to New Jersey?"

Inside the Richardson house, the family with its two remaining guests is intently watching the action, straining to catch every word.

"That, sir, is supposed to be a closely guarded secret," the colonel retorts.

He calls to two nearby soldiers, who come running at his command, and orders that the NNN correspondent be taken into custody, and marched to the tent of the commanding general.

The colonel storms off, leading the way to a third tent a short distance away, with ET and his captors following behind him.

Unknown to all but Ethan Thomas they are also followed by the *System*.

Opening the flap of the tent, the officer wordlessly signals to his three followers to wait for further directions.

He lowers the flap behind himself; then moments later he reappears.

He beckons the guards to bring the correspondent into the general's tent.

Ethan Thomas of National News Network is ushered into the presence of the great man himself, George Washington.

Close on the heels of ET is Lyndsey, 'intruding' the *System* right into the tent, continuing the family's coverage of the event.

Resplendent in his dress uniform, and looking nothing like his currency portrait, the general orders Thomas to be searched for weapons.

Naturally, of course, nothing is found. His digital camera, the little metal box, is ignored, as no one knows what it is and it remains in Ethan's pocket.

"You asked Colonel Sewell for a statement concerning a crossing of the Delaware River.

"Tell me," he asks politely, yet with authority in his voice, "how do you know about our intention to cross the river?"

Ethan licks his lips to relieve his nervousness, and then takes the bull by the horns. "I saw a newspaper article about it, sir," he murmurs.

"What! No one is supposed to know about this operation," he asserts.

"How can we carry on a campaign against the British if newspapers are being given information and publishing it in advance of my actions?" he rails bitterly.

"Who are you, sir? What is your name?"

"I am Ethan Thomas, of the National News Network. I'm gathering news concerning the Continental Army's strategy against British forces in New Jersey.

"I was given a great deal of helpful information by the publisher of the *Philadelphia Mercury*, Mr. Benjamin Fraser."

"I know Ben Fraser. He wouldn't have given you any information about my movements. He's a supporter of our cause.

"How dare you use my friend's name in an endeavor to trick me?" the general demands.

"I'm not trying to trick you, General Washington. Look! I have a special drawing of Mr. Fraser that I made of him just yesterday," the journalist said, slipping out his camera.

Colonel Sewell edges a hand toward his flintlock pistol, as Ethan dips into his right-hand pocket.

As the camera surfaces, he relaxes his grip, as the digital device does not have the appearance of a firearm.

Thomas flips the electronic device over and shows the general the screen on the back.

He powers it up and selects replay and the image that appears on the screen is Washington's friend, Benjamin Fraser, newspaperman, of Philadelphia fame.

What a lifesaver. Reacting in the same way as had Ben Fraser, Washington's jaw hangs down in shock at the sight on the screen.

"That is an excellent likeness, Mr. Thomas. Ben looks so real, it's as if he's moving!"

"This is a special box that helps me to make accurate drawings very quickly."

"General, may I have it make a drawing of you, sir?"

Washington's chest suddenly gets bigger, as he draws his stomach in tight: "Of course, sir."

ET aims the camera, triggers about five seconds of footage, then quickly switches the camera back to its replay mode, and shows Commanding General George Washington the results.

The future President of the United States of America looks with fascination at the screen, and then invites Colonel Sewell to view it. Just like the general when he first saw the video of Benjamin Fraser, down went his jaw.

"Can you tell me where I could get such a device for my own use?" the general enquires.

"It's a new invention that is not yet ready for sale," Thomas states. "Could I write you, and let you know when, where, and how you could obtain one?"

"Yes, please do," George W. responds. "I'll give you some details of the action, Mr. Thomas, but you must promise not to publish it until after the operation is completed.

"Will you agree to keep this information to yourself for now, Mr. Thomas?" The general's 6' 2" height gives him a statuesque appearance beside the news anchor's 5' 10".

"My lips are sealed, sir. I appreciate your confidence." ET is happy that it looks as if he isn't going to be in any further hot water.

"My plan is to use the boats presently on the river to cross over the Delaware at midnight tomorrow.

"Following that, we'll march down to Trenton to take on the Hessians, German mercenaries, hired by the British to keep us out of New Jersey.

"You must forgive me, but I have much to do to prepare for the action tomorrow. Colonel Sewell will return you to the place where he found you."

"Thank you, General Washington. You've been most kind," ET says as he shakes hands with the real George Washington and bids him a "good day."

"Colonel Sewell," Ethan says, as they leave the tent. "Could I get a drawing of you too, just so that I don't forget your face?"

Stomach in, chest out; same old story. Ethan makes about five seconds of video of the colonel, too, and then displays him the on-screen results.

Sewell is amazed. Never again in his lifetime will this man ever see video of himself, in the middle of the Revolutionary War, or any other time or place for that matter.

The correspondent accesses the house once more by way of the time portal.

He very graciously accepts the congratulations of all those in the family room for his diplomacy and skill in worming his way around the general.

"OK, Lynz. Now we have to do a little bit of time shifting. Could you move us ahead in time about 30 hours?" DJ asks.

Now, Lyndsey moves forward in time until one entire night passes, and then gently eases her way through the morning of December 25, and most of the afternoon of the same day.

The watch continues to confirm that the date and time are correct.

In the meantime, the movement of the encamped Continental Army is in the general direction of the river, at the location known as McConkey's Ferry Inn.

During the daylight period, some 25 to 30 flat-bottomed industrial boats, to be used for the crossing of the river, are brought to the site. The boats are normally used for the transportation of pig iron.

General Washington and his council of war are reported to be meeting at homes in Newtown, PA, during the strategic planning for the crossing, which is viewed by many historians and military strategists to be a stroke of genius.

Historically, the group knows that things are not going well in the war with the Brits, and, even on this date in 1776, the situation continues to look very grave for the Continental Army.

Unfortunately, the weather continues to deteriorate as midnight approaches.

Rain, hail, sleet and snow ceaselessly plague the troops. The seemingly endless precipitation is going to make the crossing not only difficult, but also very discouraging.

General Washington has singled out a section of his American soldiers from Massachusetts, with a background in the boating and fishing industries.

These men have been selected to care for the job of poling the boats across the river.

Strategically, in waiting for darkness, Washington will be enabled to manage the maximum surprise.

His next problem is that he has to get across the river.

Some time later, about 2:00 a.m., the army collects at the river's edge and boards the boats in squads of six to eight men, approximately forty men per boat, not including four men to power each vessel.

The Massachusetts' men are able stand inside what the local populace would call a Durham boat, with the rim of the boat at above waist level, and push the boat with long poles.

The remaining two boatmen can use longer poles pushed into the riverbed and propel the boat forward by walking along the boat's rim, wide enough to provide space on each side of the vessel for such operations.

All the while they must maintain a bi-directional pressure (both downward and aft), on the poles.

Some boats are bigger and some smaller, and can take more, or less men. None is fitted with seats, so all have to stand, including General Washington himself, in the first boat.

Contrary to what is indicated in the famous painting of the event, the stars and stripes of the American flag are unable to fly over any of the boats.

History has told the family and its guests that the design and manufacture of Old Glory are still more than a month in the future.

The Durham boats ply the river, roughly two hundred and fifty yards wide, back and forth, to and fro, until most of the 2,400 men are standing on the east bank of the Delaware.

Despite the adverse effects of the ice, rain, sleet, and snow, the crossing is successful, thanks to the courage and persistence of the men.

Once the soldiers are transported, a regular ferryboat is used for the transfer of the artillery, horses, and supplies, from the Pennsylvania side over to New Jersey's shore.

With the men safely ensconced on the eastern side of the river, they receive no welcome from the British Colony of New Jersey

This organization remains totally unaware of the arrival of two thousand, four hundred soldiers of the Continental Army, who now face a ten-mile hike to Trenton.

The soon-to-be hero, George Washington, will elect to have his men regroup, then march down two parallel roads.

Half of the men will travel down Pennington Road, the remainder down River Road, to the outskirts of the Town of Trenton.

Awaiting the Continental Army there is a British garrison of 1,400 Hessian mercenaries, positioned by the British Army to repel attacks by General Washington's troops.

Amazed, the family and its guests watch in awe.

The march is over somewhat after 6:00 a.m., and, starting within about two hours, on December 26, 1776, the Colonials open fire on, and rout the Hessians.

The entire affair lasts but forty-five minutes, and Washington's men are able to take nine hundred Hessians as prisoners from the garrison.

The tired, hungry Americans are delighted to find food, supplies, and especially, ammunition.

Without pursuing the General any further on this occasion, history records that, building on his Trenton success, the Americans march onward toward Princeton, where they again defeat the British a few days later.

Victories at the two New Jersey locations are sufficient to drive the British out of New Jersey.

Together, they give the fledgling Continental Army, and the people of the American colonies, a huge sense of achievement, and a great deal of impetus, as they continue in their fight against the tyranny of the British throne.

Ultimately, in 1783, the fighting is over and a peace agreement becomes a reality, resulting in the total disbandment of the Continental Army.

As always, the entire operation has been captured on DVD.

"What did you think of that trip, Ron?" Ethan asks his producer.

"Wow! That's hard to believe! … How do you handle the questions people raise about your traveling back in time to their day? … What else have you folks seen?" Pfeffer asks.

"Well, to be honest, nobody has ever asked where we are from. Ethan has seen video of most of the locations we've been able to visit.

"Iwo Jima back in 1945; Ie Shima off Okinawa, that same year.

"The kids crossed the Atlantic Ocean and found Christopher Columbus sailing the wrong way on his 'voyage of discovery' back in 1492.

"On that same occasion a trip was made over to the Tower of London to find someone who would have an accurate idea of the date in 1492, because most folks back then didn't bother with calendars.

"Ethan found us because he took the initiative to follow up on some loose-lipped comments. That was while we were solving a problem some people had in a mine in Paw Paw, West Virginia.

"We made the same mistake at a high-rise fire in Boston a couple of weeks ago."

Ron nods his agreement. "Yes," he says, "ET mentioned those two events to me, as well as some of your World War II exploits. How limited are you in where you can go?" he asks.

Russell redirects the question to James. "DJ, would you like to answer that one?"

"Well, Ron," James takes over, "that's an excellent question. Truthfully, we don't know of any limitations on the extent to which we can use the *System*.

"We've been back to 1492, both in the western Atlantic and to London.

"We just got home from a successful trip back to 1776 without any difficulty.

"Travel-wise in the real-time mode, we've been to Australia; Boston; West Virginia; Oceana Naval Air Station in Virginia, as well as all over the Tampa Bay area.

"In many of those places, and even back in 1492, we were able to interact with people without any apparent hitch.

"Several times in the Okinawa area, we were able to take walks outside the *System*.

"It looks as if we can go to pretty much any point in time without any difficulty, as long as that time is behind us.

"Ethan asked us yesterday what we had done about time-travel into the future, and my dad told him that we haven't done anything about it.

"As a family, we're very concerned about the possibility of making a change to something over which we have no control and that might jeopardize history."

Pfeffer, "George Washington crossing the Delaware was a great choice for us all, because we all learned about that in grade school, but what other destinations have you thought about?

"I'm just thinking about some hot spots that would interest our NNN audiences for Ethan's programs in the days ahead."

"Well," James continues, "we've got our eye on the California '49ers.' No, not the football team, but the prospectors of the 1848 gold rush.

"They came to be called '49ers,' because the thousands who came from other parts of the world only arrived in California in 1849. Even I'm looking forward to that one.

"Too, other suggestions we've had are, visit Windsor Castle in England to see the doll's house that the people of Britain gave to Queen Mary.

"It was given as a tribute to the royal family after World War I. Mary was the wife of King George V.

"The doll's house was presented to her in 1925. The ladies here all have expressed a great interest in seeing that.

"Someone else suggested Tombstone, Arizona, to see Wyatt Earp and his brothers, and Doc Holliday, take on the Clanton brothers and the McLowery boys, in the gunfight at the OK Corral.

"Maybe we could get some good footage the nineteenth century guys weren't able to get from their old cameras."

"What thoughts have you had, Ethan?" the teen asks.

"Well, now that you come to mention it," Ethan raises the question, "what would be the possibility of getting into that White House conference back in 1972?

"We might be able to record video of President Nixon giving instructions to hire the Watergate burglars.

"Maybe we could get some genuine footage of Lyndon Johnson receiving recommendations from his advisers about the Gulf of Tonkin in 1964, which got the United States so heavily committed to the Vietnam War."

"I think we can all see where *your* interests lie, ET. How about you, Ron?"

"Well, I always like to look for stories that appeal to a wider audience, and some of your ideas certainly would do that.

"Myself, I'd be likely to go for a trip over to see the Battle of the Little Bighorn, Custer's last stand.

"Or, perhaps, because the movie about Pearl Harbor was so successful fifteen or so years ago, it might make an appealing show for Ethan if we took a trip back to December 7th, 1941, to see what really happened.

"Maybe even another visit to the White House, to find out what President Roosevelt really knew in advance of the Japanese attack.

"Some of these have been extremely contentious questions that have been bothering journalists for decades. They would be a real coup for Ethan."

"Can I get a suggestion in here?" Jackie Grover asks.

"Sure, Grandma Jay, go right ahead!"

"Rosa Parks died ten years ago, and I thought it would be nice to make a live trip back to the mid-1950s incident on the bus that brought her to national prominence.

"Also, at least two of us ladies here have an interest in getting some accurate information about Susan B. Anthony."

There was no need for Jackie to enlarge on either of those two famous women. Their names are still household words throughout the United States.

"If you're taking other suggestions," Pop Grover added from beside his wife, "I would like to add a trip to two American pioneers from the nineteenth century.

"One is Thomas Edison, and the other is Alexander Graham Bell; they would be very educational trips.

"On top of that, I have always wondered what life would have been like under Roman rule. I'd love to go back in time and see that.

"Too, how could we not go back to the Alamo and see another great moment in American history?"

####

10 'Franchising' by Alex Allca

As the conversation dies down, Alexander Allca now raises the matter of the willingness of the family to lease out the technology that had so mysteriously fallen into its collective lap.

"What thought have you given to making an enterprise out of this technology?" the Philadelphian inquires.

Interestingly, he indicates that 'off the top of his head' he can come up with the names of many companies that could unquestionably benefit from the unprecedented capabilities of the System.

He adds that, too, there are many government agencies that would appreciate a functionality of this kind.

Russell counters with a caution the family has felt, regarding the need to protect the System, citing the possibility of being able to clone other sets.

"How would we go about preventing purchasers from creating other HDTVs with the travel capability and selling them?" he queries.

"What could we do to stop them from handing portals over to unscrupulous individuals who want to use the *System* for wrong ends?"

He explained his concern that an unscrupulous 'operator' could 'cruise' into the U.S. Mint, and strip it of a small fortune, with no one any the wiser.

The same potential would exist for Fort Knox, permitting a user to help himself or herself to some of the gold Monday to Friday after working hours. There is no way to prevent that.

"What about a foreign power that wants to bankrupt the United States?

"Using the System the criminals could help themselves to a day's production of $20 bills at the mint, replacing them with counterfeit notes. Can you see Uncle Sam asking for Chapter 11?"

"It's easy to understand your concern, Russ." Allca had no criticism, seeing Russell's concerns as genuine risks.

However, Alex does wish Russ and the family to take some action with the miraculous powers that have suddenly landed on the family's doorstep.

Alex begins with a brief history lesson. "Remember, Russ. How did Winston Churchill handle the issue of security related to the Axis ciphers?

"The British developed code-breaking computers to crack the German Enigma cipher. The British called the messages Ultra.

"Churchill had Hitler's Ultra signals under close observation at all times, using trustworthy teams of men especially chosen for the task.

"It could be anywhere in the world that someone approved by Churchill to receive this top secret information could be located.

"So, Churchill had a crew of hand-picked men specially selected and trained to receive that traffic, and to hand it to that one individual, to insure the Ultra secret never got out.

"His plan was hyper-successful. The extremely crucial secret data was almost never handed to anyone whose name was not on Churchill's list.

"For the vast majority of the people of the world, it came as an absolute shock when the news of the Ultra secret was released to the general public in 1974, after over thirty years.

"The bottom line to all of this is to simply use the same procedure Winston used.

"Provide each *System* with a person of absolute integrity, an *Untouchable*, a person you have personally vetted to insure his or her integrity.

"What I am proposing is that the family should *lease* the equipment; not sell it. That way, it always remains your property.

"The client must agree to have your *Untouchable* operator use the unit only within the guidelines that you provide. If he refuses your terms, you leave!

"Remember, you only need to unplug the unit from the power supply and it's just another TV set.

"The lessee must provide a climate-controlled, blast-proof, bulletproof room which can only be accessed with permission from the *Untouchable* inside, with CCTV covering all access routes.

"Each unit must be placed in that closed environment; controlled from a console that is absolutely secure. Only one person has the entrance key and password.

"Remember what I said before, the *Untouchable* (and he is allowed to have other *Untouchables* as assistants,) handles every operation for the client, if that transaction is genuine and within parameters that you will provide.

"That will give you absolute control over the end-users of your equipment. You'll be doing virtually everything instead of them. They never get to touch the *System*."

"Well, as I said to the family the other day, this is an interesting thought," Russell replies. "Lynz and Deej were bantering back and forth about some sort of a courier service using the portal.

"The thing is, we don't even have the resources to mount an operation like that."

"Frankly, we can easily agree that this is an incredible idea, but we can't afford to do very much, even with the extended families kicking in with some support.

"We would be stretching our credibility at the bank by asking for a loan anywhere near the size we would need, even taking out a second mortgage on the house," Russell states.

Alex continues, "I'll tell you what. This technology has to be of greater use than for entertaining trips into the past to see John

Summerfield at the Tower of London, James W. Marshall, and Tom Edison, as enjoyable as they are.

"What is needed is to launch this project on an urgent basis.

"There is a way to put this technology to work in getting some work done toward cleaning up this country.

"What I mean is in the sense of helping ordinary people, not only in a time of emergency, such as Paw Paw and the Mass Tower incident.

"But, rather, cutting back on the corruption and criminal activity, benefiting the entire population through the use of the *System*.

"I like the way you all act. You're unusual as a family. You all get along well and you obviously stand by what you believe; you've even raised your children to the same standards as you stick to yourselves.

"So, I'll tell you what we can do.

"I'll make a gift to you of the funds you need to get things going. The Allca Foundation will start you off with a $20 million grant and I'll stand you anything you need beyond that.

"I'm very impressed with your integrity, Russell, and should commend you for it, all of you," Allca volunteered.

"By the way, I do expect that every one of you that works for the organization will receive an excellent salary, with full benefits, the equivalent of the staff at the Allca Foundation, both for the salary and the fringe benefits.

"If this is OK with you, I'll set my legal department to work on getting you set up as a non-profit organization, with you as the president, Russell.

"Let me know what positions you want to assign to Dianne and all four of your parents, if they decide they would like to get involved.

"Include Lyndsey and James as soon as they legally can be recruited. They can be vice-presidents. Perhaps you could check out how to set them up with home schooling so that they can be available in the event that things get exciting.

"If they're too young to hold corporate positions, let them serve as department heads, or managers, and pay them handsomely, too.

"Let me know what you would like to use as a name for the organization."

"This is amazing! I don't know how to respond. It's tremendously generous of you, Alex. What a marvelous opportunity you're putting before all of us.

"ET, what do you think?"

"Good for you guys, Russell," the correspondent congratulates.

"I just need you to say that NNN can have the exclusive first broadcast rights for all video made of the operations your *Untouchables* handle for you at any of the companies that take out franchising leases from you."

Laughing and winking, Russell replies, "Have your people get hold of my people and we'll talk about it."

"Thinking about that, though, ET, there might be some question as to privacy and security if there are sensitive issues, but I guess we can cross that bridge when we come to it," Russ mentions.

"Dad, what do you think?" Russell questions his father, Buckminster Richardson.

Buck and Ladybird, having had a whispering session during the discussion, have already made up their minds. "Listen, we're in for the long haul.

"This is an awesome opportunity for you, even all of us, to leave a genuine mark on the world stage, especially if, as Alex said earlier, something can be done about taking our country back from the bad guys."

"Pop, Jay, what's your take on this." It is now the turn of Dianne's parents. Again, there is no hesitation.

"We're still plenty young enough to be able to handle this for quite a few years. I hope the System keeps plodding on the way it is now and doesn't fade out on you."

"That's one of the first areas we have to look seriously at. It would be a disaster if somehow we lost our connection with whatever cause it is that's driving this effect," Russell adds.

Allca concludes, "Then, hopefully, we're agreed on this.

"I have to get the legals at the Allca Foundation to do the necessary with your lawyer, and work out the details of how to have the papers drawn up to cover the grant, and the setup of the non-profit organization.

"Then we can get the cash on its way to you.

"By the way, don't plan on working out of the house for too long. You simply won't have the room.

"Perhaps you'd be good enough to arrange the first meeting of the Board of Governors and decide what positions everyone will be assuming.

"I'll need you to call me and let me know the results of that, and also the name you want to give to the organization.

"Since your parents on both sides are willing to share in the activities, you might think about the possibility of having them be your first *Untouchables*, which will save any conflict in getting your early contracts up and running.

"Although they might be assigned to work out-of-town, you can always keep in instant touch with them using a small screen HDTV hooked up to the System.

"Would you be good enough to have your family lawyer check out the home-schooling I suggested for the two young ones? My legals will check on the age at which they will become eligible to hold corporate positions.

"Even if it's not for a year or two, that shouldn't be any impediment; you can just use them and we'll make any necessary adjustments to the arrangements when they are of age.

"They certainly should be included in all the activities to the extent possible; after all, James was the original time-traveler and, from what you've told me, Lyndsey wasn't far behind.

"I guess she was pretty ticked off at him when she found the shot-up chesterfield and James the only body in sight, with a silly grin on his face, saying 'a U.S. marine did it.'"

After the laughter dies down, Buckminster offers to make coffee for everyone and the crowd moves upstairs to the kitchen at his call.

#

"Russell," Alex asks, "give me an idea how you would proceed if, say the St. Pete's police department called you up and asked you if you could help them to solve a certain crime?

"Say, for example, the son of the chief of police has been kidnaped and is being held for ransom by some criminal types, who are asking $1m or he will be killed.

"How would you go about being of help?"

"I love this stuff," Russell gushes. "Perhaps Dianne could answer this."

"Wow," Dianne says, "This is just like the situation the kids handled with the kidnaped girl in Toronto.

"They had a simple solution: They just went to Toronto, found the girl's home, waited outside until she left the house for the last time on the day of her kidnaping.

"The kids followed her through the *System* as she walked down the street.

"The girl was taken by a man who dragged her into a nearby home and concealed her in a room under the floor.

"Lynz and Deej followed without being seen, were able to enter the house without the man's knowledge, and watched him tie her up.

"They made a video of the entire trip and, since the girl had already been rescued by the time the kids learned of it, they did nothing about helping her to escape.

"The DVD record of the operation was passed on to our lawyer, who relayed it on to the police in Toronto, so that they would have ironclad evidence of the guilt of the perp, and he wouldn't be able to escape justice."

"Great story," the billionaire responds. "Now, remember, we know that there is no way that we can just up and donate a *System* to every police department in the country.

"Somebody has to ante up and pay for it.

"In the event you get a call from St. Pete's police, or anyone in the same field, you will have to sell them on the idea of leasing a 'liaison unit' from the organization.

"The point is that their overall rate of crime is going to be dropping 'big time' as a direct result of their taking the unit, which will save any city, like St. Petersburg, millions of dollars in law-enforcement costs.

"You can even use your own experience with the SUV as a demo, to remind them of the stolen vehicle.

"Use your photos and the video you produced by deploying your own copy of the *System* to help St. Pete's to apprehend the crook.

"In reality, you could deploy the *System* from home. You don't need to be at a police department's offices to handle that kind of query," he acknowledges.

"If anyone comes along with whom you have no previous experience, or you do not know, or suspect may not be genuine, I'll give you contacts inside the Allca Foundation who can check people out for you.

"We need to make sure that no crooked people get their hands on this technology."

Jay pipes in with a thought. "How about locating money or treasures that have been lost for centuries, say in Spanish galleons on the high seas?

"Perhaps they were sunk in centuries past and their exact positions are now unknown.

"We could back-pedal in time to find the ships and follow them until they are sunk, mark the location and hand the info off to marine recovery experts to get back for us.

"Treasure of this sort is often generally considered the property of the finder. Is there some way that the organization could take advantage of such finds?"

"That's a great scenario, Jay. Thank you for coming up with that thought.

"You know, there's a great deal of misery in the world today because of the type of incidents that you mention.

"Your expression brings a thought to mind that we might be able to alleviate some of that suffering.

"We don't need that money ourselves. Your organization will thrive on monies it can earn right here in the United States.

"What would you think of finding the sunken or buried treasure and restoring it to the country to which it originally belonged?"

"What a great idea, Alex," Ethan chimes in. "How do you think it would be possible to do that; without the possibility of it falling into someone's Swiss bank account, and being lost to the people forever?

"This is why so many of the world's developing countries are still developing, when life should already be prosperous for their citizens."

"Holy smoke!" the philanthropist says, "We'd need to set up another non-profit organization to handle that side of the operation, but there's no reason why not.

"We could simply arrange to sell the merchandise and hand the money over to charities in that country and making sure your *Untouchables* handle the distribution of the proceeds of the sale.

"If there is any interference by corrupt government officials and we can get a foreign bank to initiate a credit card arrangement.

"Each individual could apply for a card with a positive balance that could be used in any store. Retinal scans and other forms of positive identification could be built in to stop wrongdoers from making use of stolen cards.

"That way the money would be handed out only to the people who really need it.

"Set-up costs could be deducted from the proceeds of the sale of the treasure.

"There wouldn't be a need to make a profit; the satisfaction would be reward enough."

"What other unrighteous riches can you think of? Anyone?" ET questions.

"What about D.B. Cooper? Would his case qualify for that classification?" Ladybuck asks.

"Who?" most of the others asked.

Ladybuck has to clarify for those who were not yet reading the mail at that time

"D. B. Thomas was the name of a man who hijacked a U.S. commercial airliner in this country in the early seventies. He was paid about $200,000 as a ransom, and jumped out of the plane using a parachute.

"Neither he nor the majority of the money was ever found.

"Some years later a young boy found about $6,000 two inches below the water of a river near Vancouver, Washington. The decaying bills were later proven part of the ransom money paid to Cooper."

"Fascinating story," is the common response from those in the crew who are unaware of the 1971 incident.

'Judge' Alex Allca makes his ruling, "There's probably no way that it could match our principal criteria.

"If the one who forked out the ransom is a commercial airline, its corporation can lease a 'liaison unit' and we can check its problem out.

"There are no poor people involved in this case, who have lost the money, and need to get their hands on it again.

"The ransom was only $200,000 anyway, and that likely won't be worth the time and effort to them, after this amount of time.

"I guess that rules out bank robberies too, unless it involves 'safety deposit boxes.' This would affect individuals, and not a corporate body.

"The banks or the city cops can afford to take out a contract with you to have you check out their robberies using the System.

"Inquiries about unsolved crimes will have to be directed to police departments in the cities where the action took place.

"Cities can afford to pony up the funds to contract you for your *Untouchables* to handle their cold-case files.

"The same goes for airlines, ocean lines, transport companies, even governments.

"This organization is being set up to with the idea of providing help for little people, not corporate giants who can afford to pay to recover their losses, so let them do that.

"Just keep those thoughts in mind, and you can't go far wrong," he concludes.

"Sorry, I forgot to offer you any assistance you need in the human resources area. We have a need to be careful over at the Allca Foundation over just whom we will employ, too.

"If you have someone you think might make a good *Untouchable*, but you're not quite sure of them, we can put our HR people at your disposal any time you need them."

As an afterthought, he adds, "Hey, this is your organization; I'm just here to guide you, and I hope I won't have to say any more. It's all up to you from here on in; the decisions are all yours. If I can help, just let me know."

"You've been marvelous, Alex; thank you for everything.

"We will gather the information you have asked for, and get it over to you as soon as possible.

"Your recommendations and criteria for accepting assignments and contracts, as well as for our operating procedures, are very logical and will be extremely useful to us.

"It's likely that we'll have to call on you for a little direction from time to time, but we're all very grateful for your input."

"I know you'll be successful, because you have a fantastic product you can make available to people who are in need of help.

"On top of that, you're all fantastic people; I'm proud to know you.

"There is not a doubt in my mind that 'the world will beat a path to your door.'

"The time and resources eaten up by private operations you carry on for needy individuals by using the *System* can be paid for by using the money you make from your contracts.

"You'll have to remember to always keep yourselves within the guidelines for non-profit organizations.

"Once Ethan files his NNN report about the System, that will likely generate many enquiries that will give you something to be making a start on," Allca concludes.

Russell is already beginning to feel a warm and fuzzy feeling, the delight of being able to do something useful for others.

In the meantime, "Until the NPO is legally in place, everyone has to keep quiet about these arrangements. You OK with that, folks?" he asks his parents and in-laws.

11 "This is *Ethan Thomas 180°*"

"Hello, I'm Ethan Thomas of NNN, and you're watching *Ethan Thomas 180°*.

"This evening, we're going to be bringing you a story that you will find difficult to believe. I want you to know that I am still having trouble getting my head around this, big time!

"Frankly, friends, I would like you to make sure that you are sitting down for this portion of our program tonight.

"A couple of weeks or so ago, I visited with a family on the east coast that has found what those folks think is really a miracle.

"So intriguing is it, in fact, that some of them are beginning to think that what has turned up in their house is a gift from heaven.

"Tonight, you will have the opportunity to judge for yourselves how true that is.

"It was astounding to me when the family sat me down in its rec room and showed me, live through their TV, something that no-one but those kinfolk, and the people who actually had the terrifying experience have ever seen.

"Five Japanese *kamikaze* suicide aircraft plunging themselves into an American aircraft carrier, USS *Saratoga*. If the name sounds familiar, it's because it should.

"Did I hear you old-timers saying, 'we haven't been at war with Japan for seven decades'? You're right!

"That attack on USS *Saratoga* was carried out more than seventy years ago, on February 21 of the year 1945. The location was Iwo Jima, a Japanese island.

"Remember the men who raised the U.S. flag on Iwo Jima, on March 19, 1945? The famous photograph of that event is the basis for the U.S. Marines Corps memorial in Washington, DC.

"This is that same Iwo Jima!

"That old flattop was later used during atomic bomb tests off Bikini Atoll in July, 1946. The huge ship broke in two and sank. So, for the last 69 years, it has lain with forty feet of water over the top of its flight deck.

"The world has never seen pictures of this *kamikaze* attack because no footage was ever made of the raid.

"So, you're thinking to yourself, 'How did this Florida clan manage to show Ethan Thomas that scenario on live TV?'

"There is a need for me to clarify the process. What the family showed me was not on the HDTV. What actually happened was that we were literally looking THROUGH the TV at reality.

"It was compared by one member of the family to watching events through an open window. It was 100 percent live!

"It seems unbelievable to me, but we were physically there when that Japanese mission was carried out! Now perhaps you can understand why even I am having trouble getting my head around this story.

"This is only one of the incredible parts of the story.

"As unbelievable as it is, these folks have stumbled over a way to make their HDTV travel through time!

"There in the family room of their Florida home, they took me back in time by means of this amazing discovery, all the way from today in the year 2015, backward to 1945, and showed me that deadly strike ... actually happening ... and I was watching it from seventy years in the future!

"Not only that, dear friends, but it can traverse thousands of miles in any direction, in little more than moments. The travel time for the 7,781 miles from Florida to Iwo Jima was under 2 minutes; the return journey literally took a split second.

"Very shortly, we'll be showing you footage of some of the operations that the family has shared in over the last few weeks.

"There's more. Hey, I'm not finished yet!!

"Unknown to the rest of the world, these folks were responsible for the miraculous rescue of twenty-three miners trapped underground.

"Do you remember us covering the story of an explosion at that coal mine in Paw Paw, West Virginia, a little more than two weeks back?

"In the midst of that disastrous situation, these folks were able to pilot their HDTV through several hundred feet of solid rock and coal at the mine.

"They located and loaded up the twenty-three miners into their Florida home, then disembarked them onto terra firma at the mine head.

"Wait ... Wait ... Wait ... I'm not finished yet. There's even more!!

"On a now well-known occasion a day or so later, in the space of just a few minutes, the parents traveled up the Atlantic seaboard, and removed sixty-something people from the roof of the burning Massachusetts Tower in Boston.

"That was the story NNN covered of two F-16s involved in a major accident in Boston just a couple of weeks ago.

"I know ... You're asking yourself how in the world they did that.

"Well, by directing their TV to the scene of the accident, in both cases, they were able to get the people who were trapped in the mine, or on the roof of the Massachusetts Tower, out of danger through their TV into the recreation room of their home.

"Then, after getting the TV to a place of safety at ground level, still at the accident site, they disembarked the folks back through the TV to where rescue workers were able to give them whatever assistance they needed.

"'Am I hearing right?' You're no doubt asking yourself that question.

"The answer is unequivocally YES!

"Not only does the HDTV transport them to times long ago, but when they arrive there, they are able to disembark through the television set into the ancient scene.

"They have been able to communicate with other people in the very distant past: Two marines on the island of Iwo Jima; believe it or not, Christopher Columbus.

"One John Summerfield from a village that today is known as Pytchley-Kettering, in East Anglia, England.

"Mr. Summerfield was a royal guard protecting England's King Henry VII at the Tower of London.

"The family needed to know the exact date in the year 1492 and the guard was the only person they could find who had the information they were seeking.

"Why did the people need that date? Well it was essential in locating Christopher Columbus in mid-Atlantic. No, this is not a joke!

"The family has discovered a means to be able to revert to the past when these historic individuals were still alive and physically enjoying their original crack at life.

"They realized that this story would be difficult for some to come to grips with if only a verbal explanation was given, so arrangements were made to burn a DVD of each of the activities that has been experienced in the last few weeks.

"Much of that footage has been made available exclusively to NNN so that we could show it to you tonight.

"Here, just as a sample, is the record of the view I was shown at the family home a few days ago, of USS *Saratoga* being attacked back in 1945.

"First, though, to those of you who lost loved ones in this tragic and very deadly incident, I most humbly apologize.

"On behalf of NNN, I want to say that I am sorry for dredging up memories that should have been buried many decades ago, but this unprecedented footage just has to go to air.

"Those of you who lost fathers and grandfathers on USS *Saratoga*, and for whom this will perhaps re-create bad memories, I hope that you will be as fascinated by this footage as I was.

"This story is stupendous; and I thought that this would, without question, get the full attention of those who are skeptical over what has been discovered."

#

"That attack was over in less than three minutes, yet it took the lives of 123 of our gallant sailors and wounded many others, which explains my apology before we ran it for you.

"Families should not have to suffer the loss of their loved ones over and over again. This attack was, like the rest of the Second World War, truly a tragedy.

"For the reason that NNN is deeply aware of the impact that this could have on the lives of individuals, we will not be re-playing this video on this network.

"The original DVD will be returned to the family that burned it. We have not copied this for future use.

"Before we screen any of the remaining video, I need to explain something for you. In these clips you will hear constant references to the family's chesterfield and its advanced state of disrepair.

"The first time the folks got an inkling that something had happened to their TV was when a U.S. marine on Iwo Jima, back in 1945, suddenly poked his rifle into their living room and began blasting away. As a result, the sofa was almost completely wrecked.

"The fact is, it has taken the family a long time to get around to replacing it. As a result, most of the people invited into the house through the TV screen automatically comment on the seat.

"Here is the DVD showing what transpired down the mine at Paw Paw, West Virginia, less than a month ago.

"I met many of these miners. They figured they were goners; most of them told me they were pretty sure they had been rescued by a team of angels.

"They had more or less resigned themselves to the idea that they were not going to make it out of that coalface tunnel alive.

"Notice how the men comment on the daybed.

"We don't mind screening this video for you, since, fortunately, it has a happy ending."

#

"Now we're going to show you the record that was kept of the assistance rendered to those trapped on the upper floors of the Mass Tower in Boston after the F-16s hit the high-rise office building.

"The sofa comes in for a mention several times here."

#

"Next, we're going to see the visit to the Tower of London and the conversation with John Summerfield of the King's Royal Guard as he gives our benefactors the information they seek about the exact date at the time of their trip to London, back in 1492.

"You'll immediately notice the man's uniform appearance, but this is explained in the lead-up to the conversation with the soldier.

"Do take careful note of the verbal interchange between the family and the soldier, Private Summerfield. You'll catch an unusual reference here to the shot-up loveseat."

#

"Following the expedition to the Tower, the family was able to locate Christopher Columbus in the western Atlantic Ocean. Incredibly, the teens were able to calm his fears and re-direct the navigator to get him back on course.

"He was actually traveling in the wrong direction and the kids had to set him straight as to which way he should be heading. Even explorer Columbus notes the wrecked settee."

#

"Finally, there is a brief visit to an unmentionable Naval Air Station in an unnamed country, where the family sneaked a peek at an antique airplane. We have pixellated over the markings, to stop that country from finding out that someone accidentally stumbled into one of its airplane hangars very early one morning. On second thoughts, maybe we won't show you that segment. I guess there are not too many of that aircraft type sitting around in museums any more."

#

"It will probably be helpful to you in getting a sense of how useful this phenomenon is, if I tell you about a couple of my later visits with this east coast family. I'll leave unsaid the nitty gritty of how I found them, but I will tell you that they were mighty surprised when I showed up at their front door.

"When I first saw the live action of the wartime events of the Second World War, along with the video we have looked at during our program tonight, I realized that this was something unprecedented in journalism,

"All my training and experience said that it would take some real skill in presenting this information to you in a way that would allow it to sink in and let you absorb it and foresee what it might do to change the lives of each one of us.

"So I called an expert, my producer, Ron Pfeffer, to give me some recommendations as to how to proceed with the presentation.

"Just like you, he too had trouble understanding how such a phenomenon could possibly exist. He too had never heard of a television set that traveled in time, and permitted you to climb in and out of it. 'That's science fiction,' he said.

"So, I invited Ron to come on the show tonight to try and help you with the story.

"Ron, thank you for joining me tonight for this segment. What do you think of our program so far?"

"I don't know what to say without giving the appearance of patting myself on the back, Ethan.

"I did produce the program; but, honestly, even though I have heard the story before and seen all the video clips, I still found myself riveted to my monitor.

"This is an unbelievable piece of luck; this capability falling into the hands of just one family.

"On the occasion of my first visit to the family's home, the folks had arranged for you and me to go with them on a kind of mystery tour up to Philadelphia.

"We all traveled back in time to late December, 1776, a rather significant date in American history.

"After cruising around on the Delaware River, we finally located the headquarters of a certain general.

"You managed to interview him, Ethan and, in fact, you even made video footage of him. It was George Washington, Commanding General of the Continental Army.

"He was kind of put out because you knew in advance of his strategic plan to cross the Delaware and march on what is now Trenton, NJ.

"I guess we should make a point of mentioning to the viewers, that this is over two hundred years before video cameras will be invented.

"It was masterful, the way that you allayed his fears in order to get him to permit you that interview.

"He asked where he could get a digital camera like yours.

"It was precious how you described it to him as a special box that helps you to make very accurate drawings of people very quickly.

"You even had the nerve to take down his name and address so that you could let him know when the device was perfected and it was safe to buy one," the producer continued.

"Maybe we should let that serve as a good introduction to the video, Ron."

At that, the video of the operation begins to screen. Now Ethan's audience is able to see the details of the trip, including the stop at the *Philadelphia Mercury*, and the check of the date with the paper's publisher, Benjamin Fraser.

Included, of course, is the photographic experience that Mr. Fraser had with ET while even still photography of any kind was still some eighty years in the future.

Once the date is clearly established from Ben Fraser, the story can move on to the river and the military operation, with special interest being paid to Ethan Thomas in custody, being marched off to his confrontation with the great George Washington.

#

"Now, you've seen everything we have, so far. As the days go by, National News Network will be obtaining more information concerning this unbelievable phenomenon and we intend to keep you informed as to the progress of our inquiries with the family."

####

12 Ethan Thomas and Alexander Allca

"Welcome back to *Ethan Thomas 180°*.

"In response to your tens of thousands of telephone calls, texts, and e-mails, we're going to return to that story that we related to you last week.

"You will remember, we told you about the discovery by a Florida family of an incredible ability to travel in time.

"First, we need to give you a little reminder of how NNN learned of this unusual situation.

"Although we at NNN were all unaware of it, this family was involved in two important stories we brought you recently.

"NNN reported to you some time ago on the story of the near-disaster at the coalmine in Paw Paw, WV.

"Also on the two U.S. Air Force F-16s that crashed into the Massachusetts Tower in Boston.

"Later we updated you to the effect that the family's means of traveling in time was an HDTV, seemingly capable of taking the group to whatever point in time or destination was chosen.

"The set, they also were amazed to find, was able to penetrate solid surfaces of every kind.

"By using this latter capability the family was able to penetrate the coal face at the Paw Paw mine and rescue 23 miners and transport them to the surface.

"At the fire in Boston, more than sixty people were invited into their recreation room by stepping right into the television screen, and then taken to the safety of ground level, right at the Mass Tower.

"You can probably imagine how eager every fire department and police chief is to obtain a franchise for one or more of these sets.

"Before I introduce these folks to you, and tell you about an unusual opportunity for them that has now manifested itself, I want you to be fully apprised as to the potential for this most unusual '*System*' that our Florida family has found.

"First, though, I would like you to take note of two things that have really made this family stand out:

"The integrity with which the *System* has been used; and the obvious principles and qualities upon which this couple has raised its offspring; children of whom they have every right to be very proud.

"Hopefully, every American family raises its children with such values in mind.

"Our Florida family calls this phenomenon the *System*. The reason for that is simple; no more fitting name has presented itself to them.

"They are continually looking for another title more suited to its functionality.

"If you have any suggestions, please feel free to pass them along to us by e-mail to newsroom@NNN.com.

"I'd like to propose a question to each of you out there, 'What would you have done with it if this capability had dropped into your lap?'

"This device is able to penetrate solid material, like the rock face of that Paw Paw, WV mine, to rescue 23 miners trapped underground.

"Imagine what a simple thing it would be to simply fly that device through a few walls and into the Bureau of Engraving and Printing building, in Fort Worth, Texas.

"There would be no way to stop this family from looting that money-printing bureau every week-end, and filling their Florida home with thousands of genuine twenty-dollar bills.

"These are unusually upright people! Like most Americans, we hope!

"That's why it's a waste of time asking yourselves: Why don't they use their time-travel capabilities to go back to the 1930s and invest in a heap of blue-chip stocks?

"Back then they were valued at only a few cents each?

"The profits from such an endeavor would be peanuts compared to what could be the pickings from the vaults at Engraving and Printing.

"That uncommonly principled way of life has not gone unnoticed.

"I have been authorized by our legal department to tell you that NNN was contacted earlier last week by someone very special.

"This person has offered to act as a sponsor to this family.

"I can identify him to you tonight as Alexander Allca, the prominent Pennsylvania philanthropist.

"Mr. Allca telephoned NNN, and expressed extreme interest not so much in the capabilities of the household's discovery as in the fact that there had been no profit-taking motive exhibited.

"Allca was very impressed by the selfless way in which the phenomenon was handled. When he phoned NNN, he asked for a detailed report of the contacts that both the network and I have had with the Florida group.

"When he learned of the values that the group has observed, and the principles by which the parents have raised their children, Mr. Allca advised NNN that he is willing to act as sponsor the family.

"Mr. Allca has been moved by the family's desire to use the phenomenon in order to benefit humankind in general.

"Because of this, he has advised NNN that he is taking the necessary legal steps to have $20 million from the Allca Foundation placed at the family's disposal in order to allow it to develop the *System* for its humanitarian value.

"He has stated: 'I have the greatest of confidence that these people will use this money to develop the huge humanitarian potential of this *System* that they have stumbled over.

"I have absolute trust in the family's work and know that everyone will benefit from their continuing efforts to put this discovery to good use for all, not just a few.

"Right off the top of my head," ET allowed, "I would imagine that there are many things someone in this group's position would be able to do with $20m.

"For instance, that would make an excellent start to a non-profit organization that would be able to share this technology with others.

"There must be hundreds of areas in which people could make use of its capability.

"In addition to the monetary support, Mr. Allca has advised us that he is putting the entire resources of his own foundation at the disposal of this remarkable family.

"He acknowledges that a technology of this potential will have to be given the ultimate in protection to prevent it from falling into unworthy hands, and offers the services of his own organization to insure this.

"This report is being brought to you exclusively by *Ethan Thomas 180°*. In just a minute, we'll bring you the family's response to this fortune that is being sent in its direction to assist in the development of the *System*."

#

Russell, off-camera, as agreed: "Mr. Thomas … Ethan. Could I start out by saying a warm 'Thank you very much' to you and the crew at NNN for all of us.

"The impression left with us is that you and your producer have handled this matter right from the start with a very mild-mannered spirit?

"We certainly appreciate your professionalism in the care you took to make sure that you protected our privacy; and got down to the truth of what has happened and what the future might hold for the *System*."

ET: "We thank you!"

"Yes," Russell continues, "we are all aware of this most generous offer from Mr. Allca.

"His legal department has been in touch with our family lawyer for the last ten days or so, and they seem to have reached an accord on how all this could be worked out."

"Naturally, we won't have the $20m deposited into our joint account, but we are going to have full access to whatever we need in order to develop the *System*."

"As you know, sir, we are going out of our way to protect your identity. All we have done thus far is to identify your home state as Florida."

"For the present we'd appreciate you keeping it that way.

"As you mentioned, it would be a simple matter for chaos to break out if the phenomenon were to get into the wrong hands.

"Eventually the word will get out, and we'll have to cross that bridge when we come to it. Again, we thank you for your understanding."

ET, "Now appreciate, of course, that I will not hold you to any of this, but what would you say might be the first steps you would take toward developing the *System* for wider use, sir?"

"Initially, we're probably going to have to look at bullet-proofing the *System*."

ET, "What do you mean by that?"

Russell, still traveling incognito, "We still have no clue as to why this has happened to our TV.

'Why we were chosen, out of the many millions of TV owners in the United States, to receive this opportunity, we are still trying to puzzle out.

"Our kids are firmly convinced that it's a gift from heaven!

"The experiments we have carried out so far don't offer any proof that this is true, by any means, but, certainly, things have fallen into place in incredible order.

"Anyway, to 'bulletproof' it would mean that, while we have it up and running, we would like to do everything we can to protect it and keep it that way.

"Lightning strikes, for example, cable or satellite outages, power cuts, hurricanes and tropical storms; any one of these could cause us to lose the *System*.

"So those protective steps will have to be the first things that we look at, the very first steps.

"Also, we found that by putting two TV sets of the same format into close proximity to each other, the second set will take on the same characteristics as the *System*.

"I don't know if you can picture the potential for that set-up, but, thinking about the Massachusetts Tower, two large-screen *System* TVs would have helped.

"We had only one set at that time. We could have positioned one on the roof where the folks were desperate to escape, and the other set at ground level.

"That way they would be able to get into our home through one, then step right into the second, and, presto, escape!

"As it was we had to let them into our home and try to gently mislead them as to how they got there.

"In the meantime, my wife 'flew' the *System*, if you wish, down to ground level, so that they could get out of the same TV. That certainly would have made it less cumbersome.

"We have since added that second large-screen unit to help facilitate evacuations like that one.

"All we have in the way of *System* TVs at the moment are those two large-screen HDTVs, which we have been using for operations, and two 12" HDTV units that we have used for some primitive experiments."

"What sort of experimentation have you done so far?"

"Just to see if we could enliven the additional TVs onto the *System*.

"That plus one or two other experiments with powering up and down, to see if the sets can be resurrected back to life again once they have been turned completely off.

"Other than that, the children 'flew' to the top of one of the world's tallest buildings, Taipei-101, in Taipei, Taiwan, a few weeks ago.

"We took the *System* there for the sake of visiting somewhere just to experiment with moving it around.

"I climbed out through the *System* onto the peak of the tower, so that my wife would be able to see how easy it was, and to show her what the *System* looked like from 'outside.'

"She wasn't to be convinced, though, so I went alone.

"I reached back for my daughter's digital camera, through one of the 12" TVs, and took it and made two photographs and a few seconds of video, just for perpetuity.

"I think I gave you a DVD of that visit, when you made your first visit to our home."

"Yes, we're screening that footage now, as you are speaking, sir."

"Tell us, when I saw the *System* in your home, I noticed that in appearance it is like an ordinary TV when you're looking at it from inside your rec room.

"What does it look like from the other side?"

"It's like a dull glow. In shape, it's somewhat like a window.

"It can only just be seen at night; it's certainly not a glaring brightly-lit object.

"In daylight, it's hard to see it unless you're actually looking for it?

"As an example, when our SUV was stolen from outside our home some weeks ago, without ever leaving our rec room, my teenaged daughter was able to give chase.

"She used the *System* to follow the car down the highway at sixty miles an hour.

"She 'helicoptered' to a position immediately in front of our stolen vehicle, rotated our view 180°, so that we were now traveling in reverse!

"Despite the full highway speed, we were able to take high resolution photographs and video of the bad guy driving our automobile with our Florida tags on it."

"Thanks for that. As you're speaking, we're screening the video and the photographs using a split-screen format.

"We have pixellated out the face of the sinner, and the tags, to protect your identity."

"Although we were only about twenty feet in front of him, he had no clue that we were there."

"How did your local police respond to the video and the photos?"

"The desk sergeant said that this was the best evidence he had ever seen in a GTA case. He was just a tad curious as to how we came up with such clear video … and those photographs just blew them away.

"All the cops in the station gathered around for a look. It was the best laugh they had had in a long time."

“”Thank you for your report tonight, sir. We’ll be looking out for more reports of your operations in the days ahead.

“In the meantime, keep watching NNN for the very latest news and reports of special events such as we have been able to bring you this evening.

“I’m Ethan Thomas for *Ethan Thomas 180º* wishing you a good night.”

Printed in the United Kingdom by
Lightning Source UK Ltd., Milton Keynes
141601UK00002B/40/P